True Alliance

a Book Series

THE NIGHT SHADOW

Book 1

William J. Gaskins

iUniverse, Inc.
Bloomington

iUniverse books may be ordered through booksellers or by contacting:

iUniverse
1663 Liberty Drive
Bloomington, IN 47403
www.iuniverse.com
1-800-Authors (1-800-288-4677)

Because of the dynamic nature of the Internet, any web addresses or links contained in this book
may have changed since publication and may no longer be valid. The views expressed in this
work are solely those of the author and do not necessarily reflect the views of the publisher, and the
publisher hereby disclaims any responsibility for them.

Any people depicted in stock imagery provided by Thinkstock are models,
and such images are being used for illustrative purposes only.

Certain stock imagery © Thinkstock.

ISBN: 978-1-4620-7194-4 (sc)
ISBN: 978-1-4620-7195-1 (e)

Printed in the United States of America

iUniverse rev. date: 12/09/2011

DEDICATION AND ACKNOWLEDGMENTS

I dedicate this book to my father, Robert Gaskins Sr. You are a true soldier and hero. Thank you for your service to our great nation. You are an amazing father, friend, leader and supporter.

I would like to thank God for giving me an amazing imagination, although it has gotten me into trouble at times. I hope this book provides enjoyment to its readers and I look forward to contributing to this world's most favorite past time…reading.

I would also like to thank my friends and family that have supported me along the way. Nancy Gaskins, you are truly a motivational figure in my life. Special thanks go to my wife Stephanie Gaskins for always supporting me in any idea I have. All of my friends, there are too many to name, thank you from the bottom of my heart.

PROLOGUE

The wind was blowing awfully eerie on that cold October morning, a slight fog blowing out of the sides of the wood line onto the flight line where we waited. Every time I have ever left it was no big deal, sun was shining, maybe a slight mist, but nothing just creepy. Plain unnatural is what it was. We were all anxious to see our families one last time before we left to execute this mission.

The families were huddled up on the far side of the flight line behind some yellow tape. The scene was always the same; it just gets easier every time you see it. Well, easier for me and harder for my wife. No matter how many times you leave your family. There is always a pit inside of your stomach. Aching and nagging, like a hunger you just can't stop. To the right of the Dependents was all of our gear, laid out in nice rows of three, ten to each row. Thirty of us were leaving, and I guarantee you there won't be thirty packs on the way home. Someone will be looking for that special somebody that just won't be there. One of us will not make it home alive, but this was a reality that all of us have faced...and accepted.

It's easy to say that you're willing to die for your country. Anyone can say it. Gung ho kids, teenagers, idiots...any one can say the words and go through the training. But when you're down range and the rounds are flying, you've lost three of your friends...that's when you can say the words and mean it. Not a lot of people are cut out for this type of work. It's tough, rough and downright dirty sometimes. But we do it for the families. The loved ones back home. So maybe our children won't have to come and face the demons that we face today. I look down at my watch...it was time.

I took my last tough guy breath and walked my men over to see their wives for possibly the last time. This was the hardest part, the questions,

vii

the unanswered queries that just spout out from all angles. We have to do our best and maintain our bearing. If you break down then they break down, and then there is chaos. The truth is that this time, we didn't even know where we were going. I was the only one that had the main briefing, and all I received from it was this would be an "out of this world experience like I have never seen". And I've seen some pretty outlandish crazy scenarios in my time, so this should be interesting.

I reached my wife first, who was surprisingly calm, which always makes me uneasy. If she freaks out, I get upset and tell her it's no big deal, and become irritated. If she is calm then I freak out because it makes me feel like she wants me to go. There really is no winning. Stephanie was a beautiful girl, the woman of my dreams and I had known that since the second I met her. She had blonde hair, blue eyes, funny as hell and tougher than I was. "Will, you know you could tell me where you're going just this one time, you can always trust me. I just have a bad feeling about this one, that's all." she whispered in my ear, as small tears began welling up underneath those gorgeous doe eyes.

"Baby, I honestly don't know this time. We're going where they send us, then they will send us home. Forever and always baby, and this is the last time. You'll always be my Stephy. And I will always think of you, and be faithful to you. That's too easy. Just promise me you will always wait on me," I said to her, staring straight into her eyes and holding her by those small hips. "Forever and always baby, you're the love of my life." She kissed me softly and walked away without looking back. It was the ritual goodbye. It was easiest for all of us, and I had to be tough for my men.

"Men, it's time! Load 'em up!" I yelled out as I started walking towards our gear. Just like I had done a hundred times before, we grabbed our gear, and began to walk down the flight line with our hats in our pockets, trying like hell not to look back. Once on the plane, we settled in with our weapons in our laps and turned in for some sleep. We had no idea where we were headed but it was a waste of precious sleep wondering about it. We'll find out when we get there.

I felt the plane descending only after a mere hour in the air. This wasn't right at all. We hadn't even left the states yet. I opened up the sun shade to my right and let out a small sigh of confusion which got every ones attention. What I saw a few hundred feet below us blew my mind. Huge planes lined the runway, three of them in all. Another plane looked like a cargo ship of some nature, now I was definitely wondering where in the hell we were going. Once on the ground we were busy looking into cargo bins and connex's. Weapons and ammo galore, was the gist of what we saw. Wherever we were headed, we were headed there with enough fire power to wipe out an entire country. Stopped in front of the first massive plane, my men and I stared up and then it hit us. "NASA" was painted over the back wing of this plane. This was no plane. It was a damn space shuttle.

CONTENTS

CHAPTER ONE
"A worthy adversary"

The day that I met Boe I could never forget. The rain had finally ceased and the wind died down. The sun that had been hiding for days finally decided to peak its little head through the dense canopy of heavy wood line that I now call my haven. I had been tracking him for days now, which seemed like weeks. I won't lie; initially it was food that interested me. That is until I saw him in battle. And the way he handled himself with such grace, speed and agility. He reminded me a lot of myself back in my prime. He had thick strong muscles that raged up past his shoulders, dried blood matted his short black hair and eyes... blue eyes that had such loyalty and hurt embedded deep inside. That's what stopped me from killing him in the first place.

So fierce and majestic, yet he was also kind, gentle and caring, all at the same time. That soft look in his eyes made me go from tracking him...to wanting him with me. I needed someone, a companion or a friend. And I could tell so did he. Both of us were alone out here, and being alone was no fun and dangerous. So there we were, both of us staring at one another. Not breathing for fear that the other would make the first move. We stood for what seemed like an hour. I held the most upright ridiculous pose to try and show him how bad ass I was, and I had to chuckle to myself because he was doing the same.

I made the first move. A friendly face is all that I needed...someone to talk to, to hold to show affection. Survival instincts kick in every time I have an encounter. Up until this time, this instinct has saved my life and I have been the victor, not the victim, if you know what I mean.

I slowly dropped to my knees and laid my knife on the ground before me. I took a chunk of bear meat from my cargo pocket and laid it down as a peace offering. I had been tracking him for two weeks now, watching his every move. The way he fought, the way he ate. Even the way he watched his back. Everything he did was a direct replica of me to the T. I had been waiting for two weeks for the right moment to do a proper introduction. I was hoping that when that time came he would trust me, and not try to tear me to shreds and eat me. I needed this.

He was roughly twenty meters in front of me now. If he attacked me at this point, I would be helpless and would surely die. I could imagine Stephanie being so pissed at me if she found out I died this way and not by the hands of a true enemy. But this was different. Boe walked up to me, passed up the peace offering and walked no more than two inches from my face. Looking at his features, he had to have mostly Lab in his bloodline. Maybe even a tinge of Pit Bull, judging by his square head and massive jaw line.

Now I stood toe to toe with this beast. The smell of his rancid breath was hot and wet on my face, but not in a menacing way. It kind of reminded me of that time I came home from being outside the wire for three months and my dogs Spook and Gunner came running up to me, pummeling me with affection. All that excitement always made me feel guilty. If they only knew the lives that I had taken while out on missions, they probably would have not been so receptive.

Boe walked around me twice...smelling, sniffing, and judging me with every breath. Then walked twenty meters away and looked back at me as if to say, "You coming ass hole?" I chuckled and nodded. This was a lot smoother of an introduction than I expected. I took the lead, walked about ten minutes north, and looked back. Sure enough, he was no more than three feet behind me. It had appeared that I had finally found a trustworthy friend.

I had snaked our path back towards where I had been camping out the past six months. I wanted to make sure that I wasn't leaving behind any clues that might help me along my journey. Maybe I missed a house, nestled into the wood line. Maybe that person knew of the direction in which I needed to travel. I wasn't on any time constraints to say the least, so time was the only thing I really had going for me... a lot of time.

My hair was long by this point, a dirty blonde that flowed just short of my ears. Completely out of regulations but to be quite honest with you, I could care less about the damn regulations. My eyes were blue, and according to local folklore, my eyes could be seen even through the darkest of nights. I am half waiting for a story that says I can see through walls. I have scars that range anywhere from car accidents to war wounds. A scar tells a lot about a man, but a man doesn't tell a lot about his scars.

I wore a pair of ACU digital pants with tan boots, un-bloused at the bottom. A tan t-shirt with the sleeves cut off covered my tattered chest. The only thing from home that I brought was a black bandana that I now wore around my head. It helped to keep the branches from cutting my forehead as I ran through the woods. It was comfortable, yet effective. A long bowie knife was sheathed on my left hip, just next to my pistol with the last round of ammo that I own. That round is reserved for me, if the worse comes to pass. To be quite honest with you, I don't think that i have what it takes to really off myself. I guess we will see when the time comes.

It had been roughly six months since the base had been over ran. Six months to a normal man back home felt like ten years to a man like me living in the brush trying to survive. With that being said, time is irrelevant.

CHAPTER TWO
"What is...and is to come"

We had walked for around three hours before I decided to take a break and relax for a minute. My hunger pains were becoming too apparent to ignore, and I was slightly frustrated at the fact that I knew I had not missed a single house. There was nothing out here. I laid down resting my back against a solid fat tree that appeared to be an oak of some kind. Pulling some jerky from my pack, I split up the pieces and threw some at Boe, who still seemed a little stand offish.

We had seen it coming but of course the mission was far more valuable than our lives. My men and I were expendable and we knew that. Soldiers are always expendable... it's pretty much a given. I'm glad I made my boys write their farewell letters to their loved ones. Every mission posed the threat that this one could really be "the" final good bye, and we all knew it. My letter however, was not a good bye letter to my beautiful wife. It was more of a hold on letter. A wait for me note if you will. I'll be damned if I pull a "Cast Away," Tom Hanks scenario where I'm gone for three years, she thinks I'm dead, remarries, and I come home to nothing. Not happening to this guy, I watch movies, I know how this stuff works out.

I knew the chances of returning to earth any time soon was slim next to zero. But I was going to do it, and my wife Stephanie, knew I could pull it off. I always pull it off somehow, someway. I remember talking her into letting me do this job, a two year commitment for $400 grand a year, totally nontaxable. I would be crazy not to take the offer. With the amount of training my men and i had, it was a no-brainer... easy money. This mission was considered by most to be a suicide mission, but now a days...what wasn't.

I even got to choose my own crew, which was a major plus. My men came from prior missions. All of us were former soldiers, and I chose a soldier from each one of my campaigns. Either I saved his life or he saved mine. We considered one another as true brothers. I had fought in many countries with these men; Africa, Yugoslavia, Russia, Bolivia and many others I can't remember or I'm unable to reveal. I had five men total; Tony, Billy, Josh, Rich and Skills.

I had deployed out to Russia with Tony about ten years ago. He was about five foot nothing but built like a brick shit house. We were on a security detail for some rich guy. He needed to be in a hot spot for about a week and needed protection while he was there. It was my first job and I was clearly a rookie. It didn't take more than three days for shit to hit the fan and the guy we were protecting took a sniper round to the head. We had six guys on the team and after the last round was fired, Tony and I were all that remained. We spent four weeks sneaking through the rough and cold terrain of Northern Russia trying to find a way home. Tony had saved my life many occasions along that trip. We finally managed to stow away on a ship headed for Africa. We figured it was better to sweat to death instead of freeze. Once in Africa, Tony used one of his contacts to get us to Mexico. Once inside Mexico, it was a free for all sprint across the border in a stolen broken down orange Ford Fiesta. I barely made it home, but somehow I managed. By the time I got back home, the Feds had already told the wife that I was dead, and had held funeral services. What fun. i hope at least it was a nice casket.

Billy and I went on a mission together in Yugoslavia. Nothing much happened until we were coming home, and got mixed into a ring of drug dealers that were being held up in customs. We were arrested at the Airport and Billy devised a plan to help us escape unnoticed. Clearly it worked. Billy was built like me, just a tad bit smaller, super funny and very handy with devising schemes on the spot, good schemes. He was definitely a useful person to have in the tool box.

Josh, Rich and Skills were a trio of their own. There are no words to describe any of them except for Skills...he had skills. The guy could do anything; he could shoot anything, drive anything, and kill anything.

Just name it, and Skills could do it. Josh and Rich were just two crazy individuals that never back down to anything. I have been in countless altercations where we were overwhelmed. Outnumbered and out gunned these boys always kept up the fight. They were crazy to say the least. These were all men I would die for on any given day.

America had found a planet and called it Secton. Don't ask me why but that is what they called it. It was identical in every way to earth, same ecosystem, animals, plants, atmosphere, and language. Except for the fact that Secton had two suns and two moons that were always out at once it seemed like, both of our planets were very similar. The other major difference was that the people there were more primitive, huge, very violent, and content with their lives.

An average human on Earth stands around five feet ten weighing in at around 170 pounds. The average person on this planet stands seven feet eight inches, and can easily topple the scales at almost 450 pounds. These are BIG people. Their animals are also abnormally large. It probably has something to do with all the moons and suns floating around. I'm sure that the gravitational pull plays a part in that somewhere.

I guess the thought process from upstairs is they think we can just show up, put a flag in the ground, throw up a few Wal-Marts and Mickey D's, educate and train, and attempt to make productive citizens out of these people. I still can't help but to laugh at the thought process some people have. Some will just never learn, but rest assured…it will always be repeated.

The United States finally had met their match. These people were a primitive group, almost cave man like, but they were content and happy with their ways, and had no intentions on someone else coming in trying to tell them how they were going to live their lives. Surprisingly, they were receptive and kind at first, I think being as intrigued as we were upon discovering that "other" life actually exists somewhere out there. They kindly asked us to leave after we had overstayed our welcome, and naturally, we didn't. When we didn't leave, they didn't form some politically correct organized rally or protest telling us to leave. There were no votes amongst councils. They hit us, and hit us hard.

They started hacking down our patrols, then satellites, radios, and FOB's (Forward Operating Bases.) It was good times I tell you. The boys and I, we knew it was coming. We had been in this type of situation before. We can smell a fight in the air. There's always an eerie silence on patrols, a distinct smell in the breeze, and tingling up the spine when you wake up at three in the morning in a cold sweat, and just don't know why.

Some people are born for battle. Bloodlines run thick with war where we come from. We knew it would take up to six months for help to arrive if we even had clearance to call for it. So we did what any good trained soldier would do. We made a Plan B to get the hell out of dodge. We have played this game enough times to know that when someone higher up says "we got this under control" it really means that they have no idea what to do if things go south. There was never enough time for a Plan C, so Plan B was good enough. We would have to build our own ship to get home in case the worst case scenario occurs. We found a hidden underground cave a good ten miles out and called it home. We called this place "the hole." For two months we smuggled out food and munitions. Anything we needed to survive and build.

The raid happened sooner than we expected. They cut off our power supply and came in during one of their double eclipses. No light...no loom. So we fought our way out and took to the only thing we knew... the woods. Slowly but surely the five members of my team and myself made our way back to the hole. We wasted no time. I sent out teams of three to gather supplies and materials to build a ship of our own. This was a top secret mission and there were probably only two people back on earth that knew we were not in a country on earth pulling another mission. So the chances of help arriving were again, slim to none. From what we figured they would probably shred all evidence of us leaving and forget about us. What were the chances of these people coming to earth and tattling on us? Once again, slim to none.

They started picking off my men, one by one. Billy was the first to go. I saw it happen and to this day it haunts me. I was pulling guard and saw him catch an arrow through the face when he was about two hundred meters out. They drug him away into the wood line while Josh and Skills ran for cover. Josh went next, falling into a snare while we were out on a hunting party. Snapped his leg clean off. I held him until he was gone. He was a good kid.

Now there were only four of us, including myself. The ship was done, aside from the fact that we needed a power source, i.e. some type of fuel to get us home. It's not like there was any gas stations in this hell hole, so I can't just pull the ship up and say "fill 'er up Bob". We knew we hit a barrier but we still didn't give up. I felt that the hole was being close to being compromised so we abandoned it, covering our tracks. We couldn't afford to lose the ship which we unofficially named "Dixie". Without her, there would be no hope for returning home to our families.

We needed a sufficient fuel source, and I wasn't going to stop until I found one. The plan was simple. Find a town, stake it out, and kidnap the highest elder and beat the hell out of him until he tells us what he knows of a power source. We had already done it a dozen times with the only lead being to find a man named Q whom lives north. We had gotten our hands on a crude map that might as well have been drawn out with crayons. We followed it as closely as we could and just kept pushing forward. Every town became a glimmer of hope that was immediately extinguished and usually ended with us being two steps backwards. We didn't want to give in to the fact that we just might not ever leave this planet. We had learned that this man named "Q" runs this place with an iron fist, like a president but with more of a kingship type approach. The more we learned the more he sounded like a dictator...or tyrant if you will. Apparently we were in the middle of some war going on. It must not be too big of a war because we haven't run into a single battle that we didn't start ourselves.

After a few weeks we ran out of ammo, so guns were futile. I had also lost my remaining three men all at one time. Rich, Tony and Skills were caught and beat to death by a group of men in a town just south of the hole. We had come in the middle of the night as usual, but apparently they were waiting on us. There were over a dozen men and we were not skilled experts at the bow and arrow at this point and time. Out here it's survival of the fittest, and if you aren't fit, you don't survive. This tragic loss now left only two survivors, me and Boe.

CHAPTER THREE
"Time to off the tooth fairy"

I picked up my things and struck a path in a new direction. I had to leave this area if I was going to learn anything new at all. According to my map we had roughly three clicks left until the nearest town. I still had a mission to do. If I just gave up and died my men would have given their lives for nothing. I had to go home. I had to see Stephanie. She was everything to me. Forever and always...that's what we always said, and I was not about to break that promise.

I had met her in Fort Lee back when we were still in the Army. We had both been re-classed to a job that we both felt was far beneath either of our abilities. She had been an LPN and a damn good one at that. Already done her tour and paid her dues. I had been in the Infantry for a few years, but lost quite a bit of hearing in both of my ears due to an explosion. Now we were both working in Supply.

I was driving up to the reception area around four in the morning, and saw her walking on the side of the road. Apparently she was headed to the same place I was, but she had the company of two guys. I was humiliated at the current condition of my truck, as I had just drove halfway across America to get there, so I just kept on driving. When she arrived, I jokingly patted the seat next to me motioning her to take a seat so I could talk. Needless to say...she didn't. But we hit it off anyways. I knew the second she opened her mouth that she was the one for me. I had already been in the process of a nasty divorce and was by no means looking for another woman, but this beautiful blonde hair, blued-eyed girl immediately melted my heart. And she has these incredible eyes...man those eyes just made my heart skip a beat. They still do to this day.

Boe made a slight grunt which immediately broke my thoughts of home and made me look back. He sensed something, and I could feel it too. Someone was on us. And I'm sure they didn't want to sit around a campfire and share drinking stories or barbeque recipes. Boe was unlike any other dog I had ever seen. His head was always on a swivel...always. Listening and smelling...a true soldier. My soldier. THWACK. A quiet yet distinct sound broke through the woods. Someone stepped on a stick, and it sure as hell wasn't a deer. Both of us took up positions on the nearest thicket we could find. We sank into the terrain completely disappearing from sight. I slowly took my bowie knife from my leg and moved it to my hip for easier access. I took the crudely made yet surprisingly efficient and accurate bow from my back and slipped an arrow into the notch. And I waited.

We waited for what seemed like hours until I saw the head poke up over the burm about fifty meters away. This was no ordinary hunter. He was tracking us and was not being quiet about it. I waited. I knew there would be more. And then I saw them, four of them in all. The point man was wearing a sleeveless buck skin shirt that i was for sure made out of human scalps and a necklace. I have ran into these types of hunters before. They were what we called "head hunters" back home. The kind of guy you would see out in the jungle and immediately run the other way. I couldn't quite make out what was on the necklace. Some type of bone fragment...always a good sign. His face, rugged and fierce, had some sort of tattooing on it. I won't lie, it added to the ambiance of this situation. I felt a spider crawl up the back side of my neck. I hate spiders with a passion. But this was no time to worry about a spider; this was a life or death situation.

From what I could tell, the three in the back were nobodies. They were rookies. No threat. They all were wearing the same thing, cheaply woven brown fabric that fit the body snug. The pants appeared to be a slick buck skin if some type, i want to assume deer hide. The thing that strikes me odd is the fact that the three in the back, look so different than the point man. This means these were people from different areas. Me being alive...clearly is no longer a secret.

Boe sank lower into the ground, growing ready on his hind haunches, waiting to launch. He looked at me through the dense forest and I shook my head to signal "no...not yet." Damn this dog was smart. Neither of us wanted to fight, but we both knew it was inevitable. If they reached the town before us the mission would be compromised and we would be even more lost than we were now. So this had to happen. Here and now. This is a prime example why you don't leave survivors. If I would have killed the guy in the last town, no one would have known we existed. They would have thought we all died out and continued to live their happy little miserable lives.

They were now twenty meters away. Another few feet and it would be on. I drew back my bow and steadied my aim...this was it. Go big or go home. As long as I can kill the point man then I'll be golden with the other three, especially with the help from Boe. My heart beat was racing even though I was trying my best to slow it down. No need to get excited. Just another day in paradise I kept telling myself. I hope my wife can forgive me for the lives I have taken. I swear when I get home, no more. Just her and I on a nice swing in the shaded front yard out in the country. Slow your breathing man...slower...now.

I let my breath out slowly as I released the string and the arrow couldn't have flown faster or straighter if I would have told it to do so myself... straight into the neck of the point man. And he charged me, catching me completely off guard. He grabbed me around my throat with these massive banana hands and lifted me high into the air against a tree. I reached behind me and pulled the knife from my waist thrusting it upwards underneath his throat and twisting. The strength from this man was like that of a bull dozer. Nothing stopping it until it ran out of gas. I could barely breathe with the weight of his hands clinching tighter and tighter around my adams apple. Damn Adams apple, don't ask me why it has to be so big but it is, proving to be quite the hindrance in this current situation if you ask me.

This beast of a man was still going, full throttle. I stabbed again, this time cutting clear through his spinal cord. If this doesn't get him, than I don't know what would. He held onto my throat for what seemed like an hour, but more realistically was probably around ten long seconds.

Then...no more death grip, just a 400 pound man lying on top of me. Here I was trying to finagle my way out from underneath him, knowing that there were still three of them left. I had to move quick or it was my ass. I finally squeezed my tiny little self out from underneath this behemoth and looked around quickly for my next target.

Boe was gnawing on his second guy apparently, which made me smile. Now there was only one, which I couldn't find. I felt the wind rushing at me from behind, and was able to duck just in the nick of time. I spun around backwards thrusting my knife into his thigh right where the artery should be... and twisted. I spun back around landing a kick directly against his left temple and just started throwing punches to anything soft I could find. He hit me hard in my right eye, sending up sparks of stars and quick flashes of lightning. I won't lie, the hard pressure feeling in my face after a brutal beating truly turns me on to no end. I closed in with him, pulling his massive dome into mine. I locked his head in good and tight and in a thrusting motion pulled down on his head and upwards with my knee, directly to his nose. After the third one I felt his nose break and slam upwards into his brain, dropping him to his knees. Finally. Done.

Boe walked to my side and we sat, waiting for a good ten minutes just to be sure there was no more fight to be had. After I was certain we were finally alone again I started searching the bodies looking for any useful intelligence or supplies I could use. I got to the point man and laughed at his necklace. "What a tough guy Boe. Check this out... molars...this dude has molars around his neck! And I am pretty sure there aren't any pliers around this joint. This dude was a beast. You mean to tell me that this dude would dig into someone's mouth when he killed them and pull out their molars? How dumb is that? I've heard of ears, fingers, eyes even. But molars, now that's just ridiculous. Let's move out. Night fall is coming and I want to be in that town before it gets here," I said aloud. Probably the first thing I have spoken aloud in nearly two months. I was finally me again, once again having the ability to find humor in horrible situations. Most people hated this about me, but Boe seemed to like it, and I seemed to like him.

CHAPTER FOUR

"Follow me to my world"

The night was drawing near and we had entirely too much ground to cover. It had been raining for the past week, so the mud made it a difficult task to begin with. I could see the lights from the town hazing up against the horizon so I knew we were close. That last fight put me a little behind schedule, now we can't move in until tomorrow night. I hate thinking this, but it's true. I really am not going anywhere anytime soon. I have all the time in the world.

The last incline was a real doozy, even for Boe. His steps seemed to drag as heavily as mine. It was a picture perfect spot if I ever saw one. A quiet little western looking town nestled into a small valley surrounded by deep woods. The streets were small, just wide enough for an average sedan to pass through without hitting the houses on the other side. The roads were dirt and the houses were made from mud. It reminded me of the old Native Americans back home that lived in the sides of mountains in the desert. I half expected to see Clint Eastwood come up and ask me if I could "make his day." So instead of waiting on my favorite western star to show, I hastily made my sniper hide and camouflaged my position as well as I could in the coming dusk.

One thing about this place, you certainly don't want to be caught out during the night. It seems like the wild life here was on steroids too. Must be something in the water, I thought, as I laughed to myself. However as dangerous as it is, it is the safest time to travel undetected. These were definitely some cornbread grown, backwoods folk. I remember my first night in these woods. Back then, I always traveled by night because I thought it was the safest and only means. But I learned real quickly their coyotes weren't like the mangy little critters from back home. No sir. They hit me hard and with a vengeance, the whole lot of them. I barely made it out alive, and they took all my food...little bastards. Secretly I had hoped they would catch me one night so I could kill them, and take "their" food. Man, I'm losing it, coyotes don't carry beef jerky in their pocket. Or do they? Of course not...I chuckled to myself. Good times.

The sleep hit me like a ton of bricks and when I thought I was well hidden, I bid adieu to my newfound companion and turned in, hoping to dream of warm campfires at the lake next to my beautiful wife. Too bad we can't choose our dreams. I always have to be haunted by my past. It seems like I can outrun it while I'm awake, but I'm defenseless while I'm sleeping. The memories are always intruding into my precious sleep waking me up in cold sweats in the middle of the night. My eyes grew heavy and I could feel my breathing slow down my heart rate. The trick is to stay asleep and awake at the same time. To be able to hear footsteps approaching, you can never let your guard down out here. The second thing I'm doing when I get home is taking an Ambien cocktail and crashing out for a week.

I hear whimpers in the dark which pop my eyes open in a flash. Acting out of instinct, I unsheathed my knife and get ready for the worst. I realized it was Boe. Does he hear something or is he lonely? I feel stupid asking him to come over here and cuddle. I just need to stop being ridiculous; he is after all just a dog. I finally whisper, "you hear something? You want to come over here boy? You hungry?" I pull a piece of jerky meat out of my pack and held it out to him. This time he took to it, darn near biting half my finger off in the process. I laid out several more pieces for him and patted the ground next to me. Boe gathered up his food and snuggled right into my left side. It felt good to be needed. Then I slipped back to sleep.

I awoke the next morning probably around what I would guess to be about eight. The sun had just peaked up over the horizon. It's not the first sun that gets you. It's like a horrible alarm clock. You know, that annoying buzzer you always press snooze on. The first sun comes up and hits you in the eye. You say "five more minutes". Which for the record I don't know why we always say it when there's no one here, but we do anyways. Well, you roll over to catch another few minutes then...

BAM the second sun comes up from the opposite side taking away all your cool shade. It's a cruel joke if you ask me. Whoever thought of this two sun business was obviously not thinking of my feelings.

I get up and shake the morning dew from my face and take in my surroundings. Three hundred meters below me is the town, and a small town at that. Maybe three hundred people, tops, reside here. One thing was a plus; these people all live together bundled up in the middle. Getting in there in broad daylight was definitely out of the question. In the center of the town was an odd tower of some type. I couldn't tell what it was made out of, but it reminded me of some type of space tower like the ones back home that the space nerds used to track the stars and stuff. I hear a soft rumble off in the distance. Glancing up to the right I can see the dark overcast of massive thunderheads moving back towards us. This is going to cause a problem. When the storm sets in, I can't see very well...which means I will have to move in very close just to see what's going on. This town has roughly 100 meters clear of wood line on all sides. "Looks like we're going in," I told Boe, whom had nudged his way up next to me to get a better look.

I hated going in these places during the daytime, it was next to impossible. Someone was always out and watching. There was no way to disguise myself, because I am a good two feet smaller than the average man. "Alright Boe, here's the plan. We need to find a way to get inside without being seen. We'll hole up in a house that has good view of everything, and just sit and wait. Can you do that? If you want to stay up here you can. I'll come get you when I'm done in the morning. It's your choice, bud. I'll understand either way". He didn't make any response...just stared at the town. If I didn't know any better, I would guess he's been here before. He just has that look, and not a happy look, that's for sure.

Boe walks away and starts whimpering for me to follow him. I guess he's decided to go in. He begins to lead me away from the town and I snapped at him, "No man, we need to go into the town. If you want to take off, go. I'm going in. I have a job to do." I turn around to head back towards the town, and he growls at me. Not a threatening growl. More like a low agitated, follow me kind of growl. He stares at me from behind a bush. I could feel inside me that he wants me to trust him. So I do.

We walk for what seems like ten minutes. Boe leads me into a deep thicket that has now started to slope downward. He can barely get through, so you can imagine me trying to snake my way through the thick sharp thorns and vines. I finally pull out the old machete and start hacking down the bigger obstacles. I try to make it a little easier for me to weasel my way through, but fail miserably. Just ahead of me is a hole in the ground, going right underneath a huge oak tree. It was just barely big enough for me to crawl through. I really don't feel like crawling through a tiny hole in the middle of nowhere, I'm claustrophobic to begin with, and I don't see at all how this would help me get into the town. I start to think about turning back and finding my own way there, when I saw Boe disappear into the hole. The little bastard turned his head back to me at the last second to make sure I was following. "Ok, looks like I'm going into the hole," I whispered aloud to absolutely no one.

CHAPTER FIVE
"Sending Word"

It was darker than expected inside the hole. I could feel the roots poking in from various angles and directions. Some were jabbing my sides and some were even poking me in the eye. This was definitely not fun. I reach up and feel something soft, grab onto it and pull, just to get myself some leverage. A small yelp stops me immediately. "My bad, Boe," I whisper apologetically. He lets out a heavy sigh and pushes forward. I really need to wait and let my eyes adjust, but can't because I need to stay up with my tour guide. I can barely hear him as it is, crawling his way through this snarled passage leading to...well I don't actually know where in the hell it's leading to per se', but I hope there's at least a cookie waiting there for us when we get there. I honestly doubt there are cookies, but I'm sure we are in for some sort of treat!

After what had seemed like an hour of tedious climbing and twisting on my hands and knees, I feel a hard type of flooring broaden out in front of me. "It's about damn time, now where are we?" A horrible stench of death, must and dust stung my nostrils with every ragged breath. "Where are we Boe?" I whispered. A dim light trickles in from a stained muddy half window up towards the ceiling. This is obviously the basement of a house. My eyes finally adjusted and I am able to start to taking in my surroundings.

Boe was lying down on a homemade pallet of blankets in the corner. It was awfully weird to me, seemed like he belonged here. In the right hand corner of this room was a blanket with something bulky an awkward under it. Curiosity got the best of me so I went up and slowly removed it, once the dust settled I heard a small whimper from the back of the room where Boe had been laying. I looked back at the object and saw two skeletons; the first thing I noticed was the size. They were human.

These were normal people from earth...like me. Well, they were normal people as far as their size goes. Who knows what they were like in person. They could have been total weirdoes for all I knew. Judging by the decay they had been down here rotting for at least a year, it was pretty nauseating. I can handle dead people all day long, but not coming back way later and watching their bodies rot and try counting the worms. That's definitely not my idea of a good time.

Boe walked over and laid his head on one of the corpses legs. I immediately put two and two together, this was definitely his home. This is where he came from. He had a happy place at one point and time, then someone or something took it from him. I know the feeling. Curiosity set in again and I examine the bodies more closely. I need to know exactly what had happened here. The chances of two people, dying together of natural causes, at the exact same time was zilch. After a good twenty minutes, I see what I am looking for.

The male has a huge two inch wide crack in his skull, indicating he most likely died from blunt trauma to the head. This really doesn't shock me, considering the fact that the people here just absolutely adore hitting guys in the head with sticks. The woman however, whom was lying in his lap, had a hole in the top of her head. It was a perfect small round puncture just about the size....of a perfect nine millimeter round. I start to move her and see it, a pistol. These people were most definitely from earth.

I'm no CSI expert, but my hunch is that the husband was killed first and the wife found him. It was obviously too much for her to handle, so she killed herself. This might be a good thing because there may be others like myself here. Or a bad thing, because they are all dead, which means they never found a way home, which in turn implies that I will never find a way home either. Which puts me back at the "I'm screwed" level. They had to have been here for a reason, and I was bound and determined to figure it out.

The room was in full sight now, my eyes are adjusted and I am in full blown "detective" mode. I have a new spark of freedom that is burning deep inside my chest. Now that I can see, I can tell that I am in some sort of research lab. There are desks and laboratories shoved into neatly cluttered areas of this room. I see notebooks, journals and a computer. I see a stairway that leads up to my left and decide to see if I was home alone... or not. Hopefully, this is an abandoned house.

I reach the steps and notice how much they resemble the steps that I made my wife a few years ago. I had come home drunk as a skunk after a night of trail riding with the boys. I had stepped up and put too much weight on it and that was all she wrote. I broke the railing and was laying there flat on my rear. She laughed because she is good hearted and enjoys a good time just as much as the next guy. But I still felt obliged to fix it. It may have looked like hell but it served its purpose, duct tape and all.

I take the first step and wince under the creak of the boards. I slowly climb the flight of stairs on all fours. After what had seems like twenty minutes of climbing up this steep mountain of a rickety stairway, I reach the top and slowly turn the handle. Holding my breath I pull out the knife, just in case. I always feel safer with the old bowie knife pulled out and ready to go. It was small, versatile and very deadly. With the door cracked I was able to catch a glimpse of the most amazing thing I have seen in months.

I find a kitchen just around the corner, with a can of beefaroni sitting on the counter! I am in Heaven, absolute heaven...and I am most definitely alone. I snag the beefaroni off the cabinet and head back down the stairs with a huge smile on my face. Nothing could have made me happier than seeing that can on the counter. I was like a kid in a candy store. I decided I would work my way up, gathering any and all intelligence I could find in an attempt to find out who these people were, and what they were doing here. Maybe they would have the answers I sought in a cabinet or a journal. Hell, maybe they have a three thousand gallon can of fuel in the back yard. Highly doubtful, but you never know. My mind races with the possibilities. This place may not have cookies, but I have beefaroni, which is second best. So I will call this a win-win situation for now.

I have a lot of work to do and thank God I have all day to do it. I flip through the first notebook I find and began to read through the handwritten scribbles sprawled out over the pages. It appears that the two people I found were newlyweds as well as scientists. They had volunteered at a military research lab working under the umbrella of NASA, as well as work hand in hand with another corporation named Tansa Global...the name sounds familiar. I know that name from somewhere but I can't quite put my finger on it. "Tansa Global ... Where do I know that from" I said aloud to Boe who was paying me no mind at all. Giving up on my notorious brain farts that I occasionally experience, I continued digging deeper.

It appears that they landed an opportunity to come out here and study the land and the people. I'm thinking why in the hell would anyone volunteer to come to a crazy planet, try to blend into the community, and just expect everything to be ok? I bet they were hippies. Once they were here, they blended in with the community and began to research the land, forwarding information through their communication lines back home. Wait a second...communication lines? What communication lines? Oh, my God, I'm in the tower. The tower is a real tower! I thought it looked different than the other buildings.

I immediately run to the computer and tried to turn it on. No power. I look at the back of the system and everything was shredded. Whoever killed these people didn't want anyone accessing this stuff. I remember seeing a few car-like batteries in the corner of the room when I first came in, so I scramble over there, trying to think how I could power this unit. I was no expert electrician by any means, but I am pretty sure there would be enough power from the twelve volt battery to power up the computer and antennas. Not for long, but for long enough.

Stephanie's face flashes into the back of my mind. I just need to send her a letter, a message of some sort, to let her know I'm alive and that I haven't given up. Sparks fly from my hands sending a jolt of electricity through my fingers letting me know that I finished wiring what was left of the power cord into the battery...and the screen flashed ON. I have no idea what to do from here but I am going to press as many buttons as I can until I got the result I am looking for. "Bingo!" I whisper aloud. An email Inbox was right there on the bottom. However I couldn't remember my wife's email address to save my life. I truly hate brain farts. I can have all the useless knowledge in the world jammed into my head and recite it off of memory, but I can't remember an email address to save my life.

All of a sudden the screen started flashing a low power signal telling me that I had thirty seconds until power loss. Not freaking good. "Shit, what's her email?!! SMS...yes, her telephone number should work, send a text to her phone!" I was yelling now, in a complete panic, completely complacent to my surroundings. At this particular point and time, nothing else in the world mattered. I typed in the number as quickly as I could. Fifteen seconds left. -FOREVER AND ALWAYS- was all I had time to type. Five seconds left. I click the send button, and two seconds later, I lose all power and blue sparks flickered uncontrollably in the back of the monitor. The rancid smell of burning plastic caught my nose and I notice a small fire behind the computer. I grab a blanket off the ground and start slamming the computer with it, extinguishing the flames...extinguishing my hopes. I fell to my knees and for the first time, I began to cry.

Forever and always, that's all I could think of? No 'I love you, and I'm on another planet, send help, and don't give up on me?" It was hopeless. I'm pretty sure the message didn't send, and now I am back to square one. The tears from my eyes are stinging with a vengeance; heavy traces of salt reach the taste buds at the corners of my mouth. I think it's been at least ten years since I shed a single tear, but now I just can't hold them back.

CHAPTER SIX
"A new mission"

Once I gain back control of my emotions, I realized that Boe had nudged his way into my lap and was there for me...which triggers another set of ridiculous sobs. "Sorry for being such a girl, it's just been a long year," I tell Boe, who seemed to be eyeing me suspiciously. "Don't act like you don't hide out behind an oak tree somewhere and just cry your little eyes out too...don't you judge me!"

I pick myself up off the floor and start rummaging through papers and journals not finding anything besides boring scientific research. This, in my particular case, does not pertain to me or anything I even remotely want to know at all. After a good five hours of skimming through pointless readings, findings and journals I find a safe, halfway open, located underneath a loose floorboard. I'm thinking maybe I have finally found something worthwhile!

I'm feeling a little bored and need some entertainment, so I pull Boe up next to me and we stare at the safe for a good ten minutes before actually venturing to open it. "I wonder what's in there. Maybe it's a bottle of Jack! Or an oatmeal cream pie...or another can of beefaroni, that would be nice, huh, guy?" Boe is now staring at me like I've lost my mind for a few minutes but then begins to play along. He finally puts his happy tail on for the first time since I had met him, and starts whining towards the opening in the ground. I think he is being impatient. I suddenly realized that his prior family has been lying next to us dead for the past 7 hours or so, and it was awfully rude to keep him holed up in this room, reminiscing about the good times.

I reach into the dark opening, take a deep breath and fling the door open on the rusty safe. I can't see inside, but I feel some sort of paperwork. I've stumbled upon yet another notebook. Nope, I didn't see this one coming. The only thing in a decent size safe is a notebook. No Jack, no oatmeal cream pie, and sure as hell no beefaroni. Come to think of it I haven't seen a single cookie since I had been on this God forsaken planet. I really could use a cheer-me-up-cookie that was for sure. The last thing I wanted to see was a little tiny notebook. Let me rephrase, another little tiny notebook. "I guess that's what we got man, must have been something important to have it hidden this well. So, looks like we're reading another book full of Latin terminology, because apparently Scientist can never write things in English. Let's play a game this time. I will read it and pretend to understand and you just say... brilliant. I hope this isn't a freaking love story on how these two met and got married, cause that's just getting a little old," I told Boe as he was still staring at me, tail wagging and mouth all open. I sat down back in the comfy cushion of covers that belonged to Boe at one point and began reading. My heart started racing after the first glance. My eyes locked to a particular set of numbers in the top right hand corner.

20120603

That is a date. Not only is that a date, but more specifically...there is only one type of personnel that I know of that writes the date in that format. On top of that the writing was done in all upper case letters with black ink. This guy was military. Well, he was either military or he had been at one point. I wasn't expecting this at all.

20120603

LOG ENTRY TIME: 0630

LOCATION: LV36500125

SITREP ONE:

AGRICULTURE AND ECOSYSYSTEM IS SUBSTANTIAL TO
SUSTAIN LIFE OF SIMILAR COMPARISON TO EARTH.
SECTOR ZERO HAS BEEN CLEARED AND REZONED YELLOW.
THREAT LEVEL SHOULD BE REDUCED TO A THREE. NO
SIGN OF BELVER OR ANY MEMBERS OF HIS TEAM. ALWAYS
ONE STEP BEHIND.LOCAL COMMUNITY SAYS THEY SHOWED
INTEREST IN SHINY ROCKS...BELIEVE TO BE DIAMONDS.

DUE TO MULTIPLE PLANETARY ROTATIONS AROUND SECTOR
ZERO THE LOCALS ARE APPROXIMATELY 3.2 TIMES THE
NORMAL SIZE OF HUMANS. LOCALS ARE RECEPTIVE TO
OUR PRESENCE. SITUATION SEEMS TO INCREASE IN
HOSTILITY AFTER THE ARRIVAL OF TROOPS ROUGHLY
75 KILOMETERS NORTH OF HERE. I FEAR THIS WILL
COMPROMISE THE MISSION. //NOTHING MORE FOLLOWS//

20120615

LOG ENTRY TIME: 0650

LOCATION: LV36500125

SITREP TWO:

I SPENT LAST WEEK WITH A TRIBE OF PEOPLE KNOWN AS THE "LOWERS". ROUGHLY 200 STRONG. SPOUSE LOCATED NEW LAKE APROXIMATELY 5 KILOMETERS SOUTH OF CURRENT LOCATION. CAVE ENTRANCE BELOW A ROCK FORMATION SHAPED ODDLY LIKE A SKULL. ONCE INSIDE THE PASSAGE, IT LED US TO THE LOCAL ECONOMY. THESE PEOPLE WERE THE SAME SIZE AS US HUMANS. THEY SPOKE GREAT ENGLISH AND SHOWED NO SIGNS OF AGGRESSION.

ONCE WE HAD EXPLAINED TO THEM WE WERE FROM ANOTHER WORLD, WE WERE ESCORTED TO THE MAIN CHIEF IN CHARGE. MASON. MASON IS A MALE CAUCASSION ROUGHLY 69 INCHES IN HEITH WEIGHING IN AROUND 160 POUNDS. MASON TAUGHT US OF THEIR WAYS AND THEIR CULTURE. THEY POSSESSED EVERYTHING FROM RUNNING WATER, TO BASIC FORMS OF ELECTRICITY. MASON SHARED THEY HAD MIXED COMPOST WITH PLANTS AND HERBS, FOUND THIS SUBSTANCE TO BE HIGHY FLAMMABLE. THIS IS WHAT THEY POWER THEIR CITY ON. THIS SUBSTANCE IS NOT ACCESIBLE. NEVER GOT EYES ON.

MASON DOES NOT FIT THE DISCRIPTION OF ANYONE ON TEAM TISA, HOWEVER HE IS VERY SUSPICIOUS, AND I HAVE HIM UNDER SERVEILLANCE. NO SIGN OF THE OTHER FOUR MEMBERS OF TANSA. MASON CLAIMS THEY HAD BEEN BANISHED DOWN BELOW THE SURFACE SOME FIFTEEN YEARS AGO. FIVE YEARS AFTER THE ARRIVAL OF TANSA. MASON HINTS TO BEING AGITATED AT THE PRESENCE OF TROOPS. ODD FOR A MAN THAT NEVER LEAVES HIS CAVE.

REPORTS OF LOCALS LOOSING THEIR HOMES TO RIOTS
FLUSHED US BACK OUT TO THE SURFACE TO CHECK ON
EQUIPMENT. THERE IS A WAR ABOUT TO WAGE UP HERE,
AND I FEEL THAT THE MISSION IS GOING TO BE LOST
IN THE PROCESS OF IT. REQUEST TO RETURN BACK HOME
ASAP FOR DEBRIEF. //NOTHING ELSE FOLLOWS//

20120715

LOG ENTRY TIME: 0750

LOCATION: LV36500125

SITREP THREE:

FOB HAS BEEN OVER RAN AND NO SURVIVORS HAVE
BEEN LEFT. ALL EQUIPMENT COMPROMISED. NO HOPE
FOR REPAIR. WE HAVE BARRACADED OURSLEVES IN THE
TOWER. LOCAL COMMUNITY HAS TURNED ON US. WE HAVE
WARDED OFF THREE WAVES OF ATTACK THIS MORNING
ALONE. AT 1800 WE WILL SP TO CAVE FOR REFUGE WITH
LOWERS. HAVE SKETCHED A MAP AND LEFT OUT FOR WHEN
YOU RETURN FOR US. I DON'T TRUST MASON, BUT I AM
SURE IT IS SAFER THAN HERE.

0915-THEY WILL BE IN THE HOUSE AT ANY MINUTE, HAVE
FINISHED THE TUNNEL OUT TO THE WOODS. PRETTY SURE
THAT M

I feel like I was just cheated out of the other half of my movie and left with a cliffhanger! I didn't pay for the viewing anyways, so it really didn't matter. After all, I knew the final outcome. Poor guy got popped in the head. His wife must have been out digging in the tunnel at the time, came back and killed herself. The man said something about Diamonds. We had only been here about a year, yet he was saying that a team had landed about twenty years ago. I never heard of this. You would think that an exploration like that would have hit the news at some point.

My mind and emotions swirl around the sentence of their being a fuel source somewhere close. I pace back and forth, with my thoughts racing wildly, not sure exactly what to do. It seems like my endless roaming could be over, and now I have an actual place to go. But I have yet to see a lake along my path.

This man made mention of a map of some sort. I just haven't found it yet. I'm sure it wasn't in the basement, and if it was in that computer I am going to be pissed. Didn't they know that all technology fails at one point or another? I slowly went up the stairs to check out the rest of the house. It looked like any normal hut in this area. Aside from being triple the average size. Clay walls with carve outs, presumably for candles, led my way down the hall. I felt more like I was in a mud house in the Arizona desert. To the left there was a doorway that opened itself into a well lit room. Two wooden chairs stood on the far right side of the room. I make my way to the left where there was a bed that stood about three feet off the ground. The room appeared to be in shambles. Tossed small furniture littered the open floor space along with notebooks and ripped up papers. Somebody had to of ram sacked this room looking for something.

After two hours of searching...with no prevail, i sat down to take a break. Boe came in the room sniffing the ground. "Looking like you're on the hunt for something too, hey friend?" I jeered over in his direction. I leaned back against the wall and my shoulder hit the photograph that was oddly placed on the wall. "Why didn't I think of this before? I really am getting old." I said aloud, my voice eerily echoing off the nearly naked walls. After pushing the frame to the right a folded map fell conveniently into my hand.

The paper was very crunchy and brittle. That never votes well for the guy that actually wants to open it up and read it. Surprisingly, it lay open and sprawled out quite nicely. It wasn't drawn out much better than mine. But there was a little blue circle of a skull in the far right corner of the map, south of the town. I was hoping that it wasn't too far, but I really didn't care at this point. It looked like I had to continue through the forest for a while, pass over a big river, then follow the second river all the way to the lake. Too easy, I thought. "Boe, we're leaving," I said, as I rummaged through the kitchen gathering food and supplies. This would be a long walk, but well worth it.

CHAPTER SEVEN
"You got me"

The low crawl through the tunnel with a fully loaded pack was a pretty big pain. It took even longer going out than it did coming in. Having new food, a pistol, some rounds and a new blanket was well worth the extra weight. Going from point A to point B on the map didn't look too far. However, I have come to learn not to under estimate the lengths between the points.

I can finally see the orange light at the end of the tunnel that opens up underneath the tree. The orange light reminds me that it's dusk, and nighttime is not far behind. I should have attempted to get a good night's sleep and head out in the morning. If there is some sort of war going on and it has already reached this city, I didn't want to be caught in the middle of it. "Out of sight…out of mind" was my motto, and I planned on sticking to it.

We came out of the opening on the south side of the tree, which just so happened to be the general direction that I needed to go. We tucked down low at the entrance of the passage, waiting on the sun to officially set. We had a better chance at not being caught if it was dark. The risk factor of the journey sky rockets, but I would rather get eaten by animals then beaten to death by an oaf. Right now I am willing to put it all on the line and take the risk. If I can find this flammable liquid, I can make it combust. If I make it combust, I can fly home. Wham bam thank you ma'am, end of story.

After a good thirty minute wait, the sun finally sets. We rush between the clearings, staying as low to the ground as possible. I look back and noticed Boe was doing everything I did…down to the T. It made me think of going out on Recon and Sniper missions; two soldiers' becoming one shadow in the night. Never seen, never heard. After a good two miles, we make our way up the dry creek bed and exit to the left. We lost all cover, and I realize that I am jeopardizing our lives by trying to get to the lake as quickly as possible. Complacency kills. Me of all people should know that. I realize we had been moving at a trot for the past ten minutes, so I slow it down to a crawl. I was definitely going to get us killed if I kept up this pace.

We crawl out of the creek bed and I see a good thicket a few meters off that would be perfect to take a break and listen to see if we are being followed. I lead us off around the thicket and enter at the point that was facing the creek bed. This way we can see if anyone is tracking us. If they are, I can see them following my tracks before they see me.

We settle in and I fill up the bowl I snagged from the tower. I fill it to the brim with water for Boe, for which he appears to be most grateful. I am quite thirsty too, so I help myself to a couple of swigs from my canteen. We eat a few bites and then just sit there listening and watching for a good forty minutes. Once I was fairly certain we weren't being tailed, I load up the pack, nod to Boe, and head out.

Using the sides of the creek as my guide, I am able to keep us at a safe distance. I peek at the map again...there was a picture of a bowling ball...so, I'm assuming a large perfectly round rock, or mountain. I think that it's safe to say that there aren't any bowling balls floating around the woods here, but hey you never know. I have been surprised before. The sun starts coming up before I find my land mark, so I locate us a good hole and we dig in. I'm debating whether to keep pushing on, but I know Boe needs the rest. Hell, who am I kidding, I need the rest.

I pull out the blanket and wrap it over my body. I pull out my flashlight and double check the map. I am right on schedule. I already have passed three landmarks. If the map stays consistent, then I should have no trouble make the bowling ball landmark after another good hour. It will be hard to sleep being this close to a real answer. But I have to try.

Fighting the sleep my mind begins to wander all over the place. Anywhere but sleeping to be exact and I focus in on one thing. Fuel. Even if I can find this fuel source and get it into a liquid form...how am I going to use it to get home. I am no scientist but I am pretty sure that climbing into a rickety homemade space ship fueled by an untested substance was grounds for 'unsafe'. However, the possibility of going home couldn't be untried. I have to try everything within my power to leave this land. And GeoTansa sounded familiar to me for some reason. I just can't put my finger on it.

A yawn startled me back into reality as I started to see the first haze of light peaking up over the horizon. I know it won't be long until I need to be moving again so I force myself into a weary slumber.

Once again, the sun came up with a vengeance. It was hard to sleep with the possibility of going home lingering in the air. I trust my wife with all my heart, but after a while, you really can't expect someone to hold on indefinitely, can you? We had already discussed that if I was to die in battle, someone would give her my wedding band. If she didn't get my wedding band, then I wasn't dead. She was to hold on until she got that ring back. That was the deal. My ring is still on my hand which meant she was still holding on. However, I don't want her waiting forever. I was already six months past due being home. I know she is freaking out, hell I would be. But she is a strong girl, she better be.

After a good four hours of sleep, I decide to push on. Boe and I both have been awake just laying here for the past thirty minutes. Nothing is out there. We haven't heard a sound. I pack up our gear and we move out. Sticking to the shadows is harder to do in the day light. Despite the two suns we do our best, stopping every two miles. Watching, listening and then moving on.

We reach the bowling ball by high noon. I recognize it immediately, a big humongous mountain, perfectly round. Go figure. This has to be the last land mark before the Lake. We are almost there, almost home. I stood up straight behind the tree I was at and took in my surroundings. Boe let out a bark which took me by surprise.

I immediately turn around and grab the pistol from my side. Just in time to be dropped to my knees. Something struck me in the chest and it burned like a hot iron being branded and seared into the flesh of a new calf. I can't breathe. I look down and gasp at what I see; I have an arrow pierced all the way through my chest right below my rib cage.

I slide myself behind the tree to take cover, but I feel my body shutting down. If I can hold them off and escape, I might be able to remove it and move on. Even I know this a life threatening wound and I have little chance of surviving this one. But a small chance was better than no chance at all.

The sound of my pounding heart was all around me, my sweat stinging the corners of my eyes. I hear footsteps approaching, but my sight starts to fade in and out. My breath was becoming harder and harder to catch. I felt the adrenaline rush pumping up through my veins and into my stomach. I raise the pistol with a shaky hand and start popping off head shots to every silhouette that comes my way. Between the volley of splintering arrows and rounds being exchanged the thought came back to my head. These people really wanted me dead. Sudden panic spreads across my body and I felt my finger squeeze off the last two rounds I possessed unnecessarily. I can taste the blood coming up through my throat. This is the end. The suns are fading in and out of my sight. The blackness is staying longer than the light. I can't believe I got this close, and yet I'm so damn far away. "Calm down brother, we have been here before…" I say aloud to keep myself from slipping further into shock. The panic recedes and reality sets in. There is nothing that I can do at this point. My kids flashed across my mind, playing and laughing. Me…yelling at them for no reason other than I had a bad day. My wife, she will never know that she really was my best friend. If I could only change back time, I could have beat a different path.

I can no longer see, but I can feel Boe's cold wet nose pressing against my cheek. At least I am not alone. My biggest fear was to die alone. I can't feel my body any more, and the pain is receding. An amateur would think he is going to be ok. But I know that I'm dying. Boe's whimpers are getting farther and farther away. But I still know I'm not going anywhere. I can barely hear him now, but it sounds like these punk's showed up within striking range and Boe was being a very good host to our new unwanted company. Snarls and cries were all that I could hear. The sound waves were hitting me like they were coming from a fan. Words and screams were vibrating in and out of my conscious mind.

I can feel my heartbeat slowing down, sluggishly...not wanting to pump anymore. There is no more fight, I am helpless. I can no longer raise my arms. I guess my mom was right after all, I'm not invincible. I always wondered what it was like to die. I am actually scared of death. I've got so many regrets. So many times I gave up on things that I shouldn't have. Stephanie, I never showed her how much I truly loved her. How much I adored her. How perfect she was in every way. I'm feeling somebody's arms wrap around me, which immediately pisses me off because I can't fight anymore. I am so tired. I am so thirsty. The taste of blood is thick and salty. My heart is beating slower and slower.

CHAPTER EIGHT
"Savior or executioner"

The smell woke me up instantly. A rancid manure smell that quite frankly seemed very fresh. It takes me a second to fully come to. I'm looking around, and I have no idea where I am or why I am here. Then it hits me all at once; I remember the arrow through the stomach, the killing, and the fighting...and then nothing.

Judging by the throbbing pain in my lower torso I obviously wasn't dead. I see Boe staring at me from the foot of the bed on which I now lay. I wasn't home, because they wouldn't have let Boe come back with me. I concluded that I must be still stranded. I couldn't move anything but my head, due to the screaming pain squirming throughout my insides like an angry snake.

Ok, it's definitely time for a recap of events. I remember someone picking me up. I hope I at least bit that guy or something crazy. I'm trying to go back through every minute that I can remember. I wasn't restrained, and my belongings, including weapons, are neatly stacked in the corner of the room. The bottom line is that somebody saved my life, but who might I ask?

I look at the aching throbbing wound just above and to the right of my belly button. And that is where the smell of fresh crap was coming from. Literally...crap, as in poop. This is in no way, shape or form sanitary. I don't care what planet you come from, poo is poo. I really want to punch this dude in the throat now. Of all things to patch me up with, he uses poop. That's just outstanding. "Boe, I swear if any of this belongs to you...I'm going to kill you," I hoarsely whisper. Both of us are actually smiling at one another, relieved that the other one has survived the recent passing of events.

I can hear rummaging through the closed door and can't help but wonder about my mystery savior. Hopefully, he isn't some perverted freak keeping me alive for all of his nasty not goodness. "Hey...uhm... this guy didn't touch me, did he? Like besides my stomach?" I whisper to Boe. Boe tilts his head, and then lowers it to the ground putting his paw over his eyes. "Oh hell no, you better answer me guy!" I start to yell at him. The louder my voice gets the more my stomach starts to bleed. So, yelling is not a good option at this point in time.

The room is dark and has an opening about five feet up the wall in the appearance of a window with no pane. There was a low light illuminating on the far right side of the room. Yes, a light. Not a candle or a torch. I had to be inside the caves. This must be where the "Lowers" are. The bed I laid on seemed to be made from wood with a very thick fur on top of it for a blanket. I could tell from the drafty cold feeling that this room was definitely built from rock. A small rickety night stand stood roughly two feet from my bed. For a cave room I give it a b plus.

I hate that I don't trust a single person in this world. There is just too much bad and not enough good. There sure is a lot of sicko's out there that's for sure. If you don't believe me, just turn on the television or pick up a newspaper or magazine. I cringe at the thought of lying here helpless, while some banana handed creeper drools over my luscious body. I mean after all I am quite handsome, and I can't blame anyone for looking. But that is a definite no-no and would most definitely be held out of the stories I will tell when I got home. Oh, you can trust me...there will be stories.

There is a faint knock on the door and I grab the covers to hide my stomach. It was at this point I realize I am in what is left of my underwear. I think I'm going to stop observing my situation right now, because I don't like where this is headed. A short man, just a few inches taller than me walks into the room holding a tray full of food and a cup of what looks like tea. He has sandy brown hair that covers a slightly tan and thick body. This man definitely has not had a food supply shortage in his lifetime. He wasn't severely over weight, but he definitely was leaning towards the thick side. His arms were wide and muscular, covered by what appeared to be a buckskin shirt. His sleeves, which he wore slightly past his palms, were slightly frayed. His pants were made out of what reminded me of denim. For a man who lives in what appears to be a rock. He is pretty well kept. I would say he wasn't a day over twenty five. A strong chin protruded out from his wide jawline as he stared down at me, clearly disgusted.

"So…'sup?" I forced out of my burning lungs. That was all I could think of to say. I know my imagination gets the best of me, in all reality he could be a survivor like myself and has saved my life, for which I need to be grateful. However, judging by his look of utter disgust he is throwing my way…I'm going to say not. "You're looking better. You've been out for over a week, so I am sure you're starving," the man said as he slammed the tray on the night stand next to me, spilling an unnecessary amount of what appeared to be peas. His voice seemed short, yet somewhat friendly. However, his actions definitely scream hostile. I contemplated the fact that the food could have been poisoned… for about one second. I was starving, and could probably devour an entire buffalo right now, so I chowed down.

This guy's cooking skills might not been up to par, but it was "food" so I was not going to complain. And for a guy who hasn't really eaten in a while, it was delicious. The smell of fresh poop hit my nose again, reminding me that this man was still in the room. He moved a chair up next to me and was now staring, waiting for me to acknowledge him.

I put the food down and spoke, "So, Mr. rude pants…. what's the deal? Who are you…if you don't mind me asking and why did you save me?" He looked at me for a good two minutes before answering.

"Cory… and I *was* part of the perimeter defense team for my people. Now…thanks to you, I am the only surviving member." Cory stared at me and I couldn't help but feel slightly guilty. I definitely know the feeling of losing a team. I could only imagine the anger he holds towards me. But it's not like I started this fight. So, he can deal with it. After a few moments he continued. "We have heard of you before, the lone surviving soldier that everyone in this country is looking for. The *one* and *only* surviving member of the invaders. There is quite a bounty on your head soldier boy." I quickly interrupted. "First off, don't call me

Soldier Boy. My name is Will. Secondly, I won't apologize for the loss of your men. I was attacked and I fought back. Any one of your men would have done the same. Lastly…I know I'm alone, you really don't have to run it in."

Cory stared at me, unblinking and not fazed by the words I spoke. There was a brief pause and he continued as if I had never spoken. "My people call you the lost ghost. Always roaming, always killing and never headed towards a predictable point. You see, when the Uppers want your head on a platter, we want something more valuable. We want your skills. Unfortunately we need your skills. We are tired of fighting and living underground. We have neither the strength nor the man power to surface and demand our rights to the Uppers. Though our neighbors are very primitive…and dumb at times, we would like to share the world as one people. Many of our children have not even seen either of the suns beams on their bright little faces. We were told if we found you, that we were to bring you in alive and ask for your help." I couldn't help but think if this how they get you to help them, I would hate to see what they do to people they don't need.

Cory broke into my thoughts and continued on with his speech. "I'm sorry about the arrow; he was new and was only doing his job. You were too close to the city. We do understand however, you were fighting for your life and for that reason and that reason alone…your life was spared. I am the city's health lord. So as such, it was my job to insure you survived long enough to speak to the governor and listen to his proposition. I must inform you however, that if you deny the Governor's request, then my obligations to your health and survival are no longer valid. You won't ever leave these caves again. The choice is totally yours of course." I thought for a good second and couldn't help myself from making a smart ass comment, "No pressure, huh? So, fight for you and I live. Or, not fight and die in your underground club house. Hmm, looks like I have some thinking to do, so many choices." Cory didn't even let me finish before he turned heel and left the room, closing the door a little too hard on the way out. "What a dick huh, Boe?" I grunted to my companion who was still staring unwarily at the door.

There were two voices down the hall. I could barely make out what they were saying. "Is he the one? Will he help us? What is he like?" The new voice was pelting Cory with a thousand questions all at once. I could hear Cory's deep voice cut in. "He is definitely the one everyone is looking for. He will help us. I didn't give him a choice. I'll tell you what he is like...arrogant and cocky." Who's he calling arrogant? I am definitely a little cocky, but arrogant is a little rude if I do say so myself. They continued, this time it was Cory's voice. "Mr. Mason wants a peaceful conflict, just amongst the councils. If we bring this Soldier into this, there will be nothing but bloodshed, because that is all he knows. We don't want that." I interrupted him immediately, screaming through the closed door, hoping my voice would reach the room he was in, "Cory! Come here!" I had some questions and I'm sure he had the answers.

There were too many similarities between us to ignore. Like the fact that there is absolutely no language barrier. Even all the way down to the back and forth banter or the government structure. The chance of both worlds calling the same thing by the same name is just too eerie to ignore. These people have definitely been influenced by someone human. Belver's name flashed into my head from Boe's tower. I don't know why but Belver just seems so familiar of a name. Like, I should know who that is for some reason. I swear I have heard it before somewhere. Oh my god. It hit me like a ton of bricks. Belver...Mike Belver. He owned Tansa Pharmaceutical. It was all over the news when he went missing. Mike Belver was a multi-millionaire who became terminally ill due to cancer. He was obsessed on finding a cure for cancer. About twenty years ago, he disappeared after a news conference saying he was taking some time to himself to see places he hadn't seen yet. It made headlines across America. No one ever heard from him again. After a few years the search was over and everyone said he had died. They just gave up searching. Some ten years later the company sold out and took a new name...Tansa Global. I remember the company took a huge loss in profit after the death of Belver. But if Belver was here...then he never died on earth. That would explain how these people came under an American influence in their culture.

Surely Belver died here, I remember seeing pictures of the man. He was not in the best of health to say the least. The doctors had only given him a year left to live...tops. So many more questions came rambling into my mind. Why did Belver come here in the first place? Hawaii would seem a little more peaceful to spend your last days if you ask me. Where was the rest of his team that came? Surely they died off eventually...maybe they came back home after Belver died. Cory came bursting through the door, unnecessarily loud as usual. I wonder if this is going to be a reoccurring thing for this guy. If it is, this is going to take some getting used to.

CHAPTER NINE
"Connect the dots"

Cory's companion made his way in right beside him. They looked at the two chairs on the other side of the room, and motioned for them to sit. Once seated, I took the time to introduce myself. I wasn't comfortable, and they made it quite clear by their attitude towards me and Boe that my "comfort" was not on the top of their priority list. Right now, I really didn't care. All I cared about was getting home, and if I sit here and act just like a prisoner I was not going to get there. They were going to use me and dispose of me at their will. If I flipped the table on this situation and took charge, I just might be able to come out of this thing alive.

"Here is the deal. You're right, all I know is war. I am a soldier and damn good one at that. There is a time for diplomacy and a time for war. I come in on the second part. So tell me your story. Why are you here and why are you hiding like cowards in caves? Why are you built smaller than the boys upstairs? Now answer my questions and I don't have all day," I said in my big boy voice. Intimidating to some, annoying to others but it usually works all the same.

Cory spoke up, he was obviously in charge here. "Back before my time, my grandfather once said..." "This is not going to work" I rudely interrupted. "I don't have the time nor the patience for this story telling business. We're not sitting around a campfire roasting marshmallows here. I want facts and I want them today. I want to know why you guys barely leave the cave and hardly anyone knows anything about why you are here and what you are doing." I could tell 'ol Cory was getting quite agitated with me, which was a good sign. It meant I was officially in charge. And the sooner he realized this, the sooner I got home.

"We were considered outcast and cast down to live in the shadows of the caves. I would say roughly fifteen years ago. It was right after the brotherhood showed up." "What brotherhood?" I interrupted politely and very interested. "The Brotherhood that united our people. They showed up like you did... from the sky. They shared knowledge on many subjects. They created our government...schools and power. The sky was the limit on what these brilliant men knew." "Cory, about how long ago was this?" I asked curiously. I can tell Cory likes to teach to a willing candidate because he continued eagerly. "I was real little, I would say about fifteen maybe twenty years ago. Anyways, no one really knows what happened for sure. But...People started turning on people. Tribes killed other tribes and cities crumpled other cities. There was war everywhere we turned around and for no reason at all. Mason took charge and said we would be safer if we moved. A group of people... my parents included...followed him to the caves. After a few more years we began to fight amongst ourselves down here. Mason stopped the uprising and kicked about twenty families deeper into the caves. We lost a lot of good relatives during that split." Cory stared off into the light coming in from the window, lost in his memories.

"So, why the split man? What was the fight about amongst yourselves that couldn't be settled?" I asked Cory. He snapped back to the present time with me and continued on. "Well, like I said I was still a teen. But the word was is that some people felt it was unfair to stay down below in these caves. That it wasn't right. They felt that if the government couldn't help them reach a simple goal...freedom...then the government shouldn't be around at all. They were banished and we weren't allowed to speak to them anymore. They are still around though...here and there. In the shadows,..waiting." Once again he stared off into the window as if I wasn't there at all.

"So, I get the idea of moving away for safety. But why stay hidden in the caves? Why can't the kids go outside and play?" I asked. Cory's friend chimed in. "Because we get killed if we go out. Mason worked out a deal that the Uppers won't come looking for us if we stay out of sight. We stay underground...we stay alive." "Yes, Johnny is right. We stay down and we live another day. It's a rough life but it is livable.

"Ok, I'm tracking. I'm tracking...Tell me about these visitors... did they have names?" I asked Cory and Johnny, probably a little too directly. "No, they just called themselves the brotherhood." Johnny said with a smile on his face. I detected a bit of an attitude in his voice. "Johnny...grown-ups are talking. Cory, does the name Mike Belver sound familiar to you? What about Tansa? Are ya getting anything here? Anything ringing a bell here?" I asked a little more impatiently. Cory shook his head no and continued on. "We have been trying for years to arrange a meeting with the Uppers to discuss the possibility of our returning to the surface. It's hard enough dispatching a messenger. It's even harder getting one to return home alive. This Is where you come in. Mason is thinking you can sneak your way through to the uppers and demand our release."

Cory grew silent and had a slight frustrated look on his face. Heck, I was frustrated with the tactics of these people. You would think after a decade or two, someone would grow some balls and go up with force and demand what they want. If they wanted help, they would have to do it my way and Cory was right. There would be a lot of bloodshed. "I'm assuming Mr. Mason is the governor. I want to see him... immediately. Well, as soon as you hand me my clothes that is. I also want the commander of the forces you have." Cory looked at me in disbelief. "You aren't anywhere near ready to speak to anyone. And if you do, that dog will not be in here and further more we do not have nor want any *forces*," he told me matter of factly. "Well Cory, it's a good thing you're not calling the shots here. Seeing as this is a small underground community, I expect him here in... let's say one hour. As for your *forces*, you need one and you will have one. Every great conflict has been solved by war. When we have time later, I'll explain to you some of the wars from back home, and the lives and countries that they have saved due to the sacrifices of others. On another note, if you touch my dog, I'll kill you. Good day." I pointed towards the door and Johnny and Cory left just as quickly as they had appeared.

There was no time to spare so I started looking around for my pants. It was always hot out here, so all I had was a pair of pants and a cut off t-shirt. Unfortunately it was my uniform. The ACU digital pattern on my uniform was horrible, you didn't blend into anything unless you were completely filthy, which I happened to be, so I need not complain anymore. I slowly and painstakingly put on my pants one foot at a time. He was right. I was nowhere near ready to do much of anything besides use the bathroom. But I refuse to sit around this place waiting to get better. The longer I wait means the longer it takes me to get home.

If I they want my help, they are going to have to get off their rear ends and stand up for themselves. They are going to have to take what they want by force. Neither side has any direct military structure whatsoever. If I am able to train these men to some basic standards, then we should have the upper hand. I slowly pulled on each of my worn out boots, grimacing as I laced them up and tucked them in. The t-shirt was the most difficult part as I tried to slowly pull it down over my broad shoulders and a huge hole in my chest. The instant stinging, stabbing sensation made me remember the poop. I don't know why in the hell I didn't punch him the face for putting poo on me! I had somehow temporarily forgotten about the substance on my chest. How could I forget about that? I just realized that my t shirt had been washed. A small hole the size of a dime was in it right over the poo stains. Hard to believe that little hole almost took my life. It took what felt like an eternity to put on my clothes. I was running out of time and I wanted to look partially put together when this man showed up. I have to call the shots; after all…my life depends on it.

CHAPTER TEN
"The meet and greet"

A weak knock on the door interrupted all my thoughts. I could tell whoever was behind that door was somewhat intimidated by me. This was a good thing. It meant I already had the upper hand in running this show. "Come in, the door is open." I said in a loud assuring voice. I had positioned myself high up on the chair that was next to my bed, so as to not look so pathetic in my weakened state, and more in control of the situation and my condition.

Mason walked in followed by two burly looking fellows who seated themselves at the far side of the room. The man on the left had dark hair and wore a rugged smirk across his face. The man on the right had bleach blonde hair and had a very square face. If i was back home, I would have guessed this man to have a name like Ivan. Either way these two men had been outside a lot because they were both very tan. The two saps were obviously trying to intimidate me, and were failing miserably. Though they looked to be about forty-five to fifty years old... they were definitely built like a brick shit house.

Mason walked up to me and extended his hand in a friendly, confident gesture. A smile a mile wide came across his face and revealed a set of perfect pearly white teeth. Judging by his features I would guess that Mason was around his mid-fifties and wearing it very well. He had a kind look on his face that, judging by the permanent creases in his smile line, was always there. This man was no fighter...he was a politician true and through.

He reminded me of my old principal in preschool... all smiles all of the time and full of shit. I took Mason's hand and shook it firmly. He had a weak shake. This man was definitely no fighter. I hate a man with a weak handshake. Looking at Mason's tan face and defined features,

I would say he is definitely in shape and he gets out a lot. Bright blue eyes brightened his face that was topped with short black well-kept hair. He wore his buckskin clothes very well too. They were tight fitting and almost in like a slacks/button up shirt style combo. I could tell immediately that he was no commoner.

"Mr. Will, I have been so very looking forward to meeting you. I hate to hear that you had such troubles along your journey to find us. Also…I hope you don't hold the whole arrow through the chest thing against us. It's merely business. We're really a friendly people here." Mason said enthusiastically and overly apologetic. "My name is…" "Mason…you're the governor of this…town… I guess you could call it." I interrupted him immediately. I was good at that and I could tell from the slight drop of the smile at the corners of his mouth and the twitch in his eye…that he didn't like it one bit. Mason continued slowly with a slight tone of disgust in his voice. "Yes…I see you already know who *I* am and quite frankly I have already heard enough stories about *you*. So, there really is no need for an introduction. I don't want to waste any more time so I suppose I'll get right down to it." I could tell that this guy was as fake as they come. God gave me a gift of pissing people off and this guy was kind of fun to agitate. So, naturally…I interrupted him again and finished the conversation for him.

"You want me to go upstairs and whoop some ass for you." I said as I stared into his eyes. I didn't want to break eye contact for a second. I had to own this moment. "Yes, Will. It's actually as simple as that. You see a man named 'Q' runs the uppers with an iron fist, a very nasty critter this guy is 'lemme tell ya." Mason started in still agitated with my interruptions. "You see, if…and when you kill 'Q', you will gain control of the Upper world. All you have to do is simply hand it over to *me*. Once I gain control of the uppers, I free my people. We all make peace and live happily ever after. You see, our children are sickly. They have rarely seen the light of day if even at all. It is my *sole* responsibility and mission in life to return my people to the surface where we belong." There was definitely something fishy about this guy, I didn't like him at all. "You know, for a man that looks as well kept and tan as yourself. You sure do seem to care a lot about your followers. Riddle me this…"

I broke in and paused for effect. "why do you and the Ivan's back there look so damn good…for a couple of guys squatting in some cave's it sure does seem like you get quite a bit of face time with the suns."

One of the Ivan's stood up intimidatingly and quickly returned to his seat when Boe let out a snarl. "Will, I do not wish for an altercation with you." Mason said loudly with his hands up in the air in a surrendering style motion. "My friends merely travel with me to my meetings with the council amongst the Brotherhood. We go up there quite a bit to try and negotiate the possibility of our people returning to the surface. They merely ensure my safety, which is something…*you* might want to start thinking about yourself." Mason said in a menacing yet nice sort of way. A silence fell across the room and I can see a smirk on one of the Ivan's face. "Look here." I said as I stood straight up on my feet without a flicker of a grimace. Puffing my chest out and throwing my shoulders back I started to speak in a louder more severe tone. Extending my hand out in a point straight at Mason's face with my elbow tucked in, I continued with my rant. Boe started a low growl in the bottom of his belly as he eyed the Ivan's. "I don't think you realize who *I* am. Let me fix this for you. If you ever… in any sort of way… threaten my life again or disrespect me. I'll beat you within an inch of your life…right where you stand. And Ivan…I'm about to have Boe rip that ridiculous smirk off your old saggy face. Don't test me. Many have tried and many have failed. I accept your offer under one condition. Fuel… You have it I need it. I'll hand you over the Uppers on your word that you will ensure I make it home as soon as the deal transpires." Mason had a furious, surprised look of a man that had never been threatened before on his face. I could tell he was aside himself. Yet, through all this I can see a smile starting to appear at the corners of his mouth. A fake smile.

"Absolutely…Sounds like a plan. Swell then. We have come up with different power sources over the years I am sure we can whip something up for you. But you *will* leave as soon as as you receive the fuel." Mason spoke in a soft defeated voice. He turned heel and began to walk towards the door. "Mason." I stopped him in his tracks. Slowly Mason turned around and looked at me clearly agitated. "Yes, Will." Mason said disgusted. "What can you tell me about the Brotherhood?"

"Oh Will, don't you concern yourself with the Brotherhood. They are untouchable...Brilliant...you won't be meeting any of them anytime soon. I assure you." Mason said with a smirk on his face. Turning to leave for the last time I hit him with another one. "What about Tansa... does that name ring a bell? Man named Belver perhaps. Showed up here about twenty years ago on a ship like me." I saw a flash of panic come across the Ivan's faces and then immediately disappeared. Mason, whose face had not changed at all in the past forty five seconds remained solemnly straight.

"The Brotherhood showed up about twenty years ago. I never heard of a man by that name. However, it was rumored they lost a guy on arrival. Terribly sick he was. As for the other...Ansa was it? Never heard of it. No bells ringing here...if you don't mind." Mason said clearly done with our conversation as he turned and rushed out the door. "Tell Cory I want to see him on your way out please." I called out after him. Once the blonde Ivan slammed the door shut I collapsed down onto my chair and could feel the blood oozing out of my chest. Pain shot all throughout my body.

Cory entered the room immediately after Mason made his exit from the house. "Cory, one thing sir...Why is there...shit on my chest? I just have to ask. I'm all for you healing me, but this is just uh, well it's too much." Cory started laughing. The first laugh I had seen since the base fell a few months back. We both couldn't stop laughing, apparently we both needed it. "Not just poop, Will. It's droppings from a bat called an Ambiguan. It's only been physically seen a handful of times. Its home is located high up in the mountains. We take the droppings; mix it with a little herb, mud and spices. It's a great healing agent, and I am afraid you have the last of it in your wound there." Cory and I laughed for a few more moments and then he turned to leave me for the night. "Before you go, real quick. Can you bring me a cookie in the morning? I kind of have been craving one." Cory looked at me bewildered. "What's a Cookie?" He asked. "Never mind brother, I'll see you in the morning. On his way out the door I called out, "Cory, I'm going to need soldiers. Let him know that. Good ones. Also, we're going to need someone

to lead them. I'm going to need him here first thing in the morning."
Cory grunted off in the back ground. I take that as an 'ok'. I had a lot
of planning to do and it was getting late. Even though I had been asleep
for a week, I felt as if I hadn't slept in a month.

CHAPTER ELEVEN
"Friends"

The morning came sooner than I had expected and the knock on the door made me jump a good foot in the air. I didn't hear this guy even come into the house and yet here he was knocking at my door. Either he was very sneaky or I was just getting old and have lost my touch. Maybe they actually sent me someone I could work with. The door opened and in walked the scrawniest guy I think I have ever seen; this was bad even for their standards. They must have obviously taken me as a joke.

This was not a good start to a morning. Nerdy kid…no cookie. I don't know why I keep expecting a cookie to waltz into my room, and dance on my bunk, but I do none the less. The scrawny man came in and introduced himself to me, "My name is Gerald, and I have been told I will be working with you on this new task." He came in and sat down next to Boe, who was looking at him just as astonished as I was. He just sat there and stared at me with his legs crossed.

Gerald stood about five nine and had a slight cross to his eyes. He had dark shaggy hair that covered his eyes which I was assuming were a dark brown. One word described this kid…goof ball. Gerald sat there for almost ten minutes as I looked him over, not saying a word, not looking uncomfortable at all. He acted like he does this every day. Like he just waltzes into random people's houses and just stares at them for no reason at all. It's kind of creepy actually now that I think of it. I broke the silence. "Ok, here is the deal, there is going to be a fight soon. And you are going to be in it. You are going to lead it with my help. I am not going to be up and around for probably another three weeks. So you have until then to finish the tasks at which I assign you. You will do what I say, when I say it, no questions asked. Do you understand?" He nodded in compliance. At least he didn't complain. I wonder if knows how to talk. I wonder if he is mentally retarded...I would be so pissed if he was. Not that it would be this kids fault of course, but that being the guy they sent me...come on.

I carried on firmly. "I am going to need twenty men. Twenty able men, that is. Not old man Johnson that lives down by the rock, selling pottery. I need strong men. All of your hunting party that remains, and possibly every kid that has ever beaten you up." I gave him a second to take it in. I didn't know if this kid was stupid or smart, he just stared at me. I took that as a 'yes I got you' and continued on. "I'm also going to need some maps, we need to know exactly where this man Q lives, how far it is from here, and how many people protect him. I will need a drawn out diagram of his land and the surrounding towns. I will need routes in and out of this place and I will need a group of ten men ready to go out on a reconnaissance party in three weeks. These men need to be able to run fast and be able to walk for days if the case calls for it. Can you do that for me Paco?" Gerald nodded, got up and left just as quickly and quietly as he came. I couldn't tell you if he was tracking or not. I guess we will see in three weeks.

Cory came in roughly two hours later with a plate of food and a bowl made just for Boe. "How do we know that you're not going to run the first chance you get when you're back up top, Will?" he asked me as he stood watching the two of us eat breakfast...which still consisted of NO cookie. "Well, buddy, you don't. But I do say this. Doing this for you gets me home, and I assure you that I want to be gone just as soon, if not sooner, than you want me gone. Can I be up in running in three weeks?" I asked him. I was more so giving him a deadline and not looking for his recommendation. "Three weeks and you're running again. Promise" he replied. "So, what do we have for weaponry around here? I'm going to need supplies; can I count on you for that too?" I asked. He nodded and left the room. Apparently no one wants to just sit down and talk.

All I wanted right now was for someone to come in and just talk for a while. Play some cards or something. Maybe someone to just ask me how I was feeling for a change. I knew that I couldn't leave the bed for at least another week, but I was determined to not lose my sanity in someone's shabby little hut in the middle of a cave. I found a small rubbery type ball under the bed that Boe had been chewing on. I played a good game of wall ball for about an hour until Boe and I both lost interest. Wall ball is a good game to pass the time. Trying to throw the ball and hit as many corners of the room as possible while still being able to catch it. There are many different variations of the game, but this one was my favorite.

Well, it *was* my favorite...before I got gut stabbed and now can't move around too much without bleeding. Boe gets a good kick out of it though, bringing the rock back to me when it hit the ground or fell outside of my reach. I guess Boe grew tiresome of fetching my balls and being forced to give it up. I threw the ball one last time, Boe jumped up, caught it in his mouth and went underneath my bunk. I yelled for Cory to come in, it was definitely story time. Play some marbles or something. I was going to go crazy here.

Cory came in looking quite agitated at being at my beck and call. These people didn't seem like bad people. I usually get a vibe off people and can read them very quickly. I can usually tell their intentions, whether they be good or bad.

"Cory tell me about yourself sir, where are you from?" I asked in a caring manner. I wanted this man to know I can be trusted. If he trusts me then they will trust me. I know he reports to Mason most likely on a daily basis. Besides, I'm pretty bored. Cory sighed and answered. "I grew up quite a ways away from here actually. I was eleven when all the fighting started and we moved down here. Then my dad built this house and I have been here ever since." Cory started to turn to walk away. "Look man, I know you have so many other things to do right now...but I really want to get to know you. You're stuck here watching me, so you might as well get to know me. I'm not saying you have to like me...just know me." Cory turned back around came in next to my bed and took a seat. "Look Will, My Mom and Dad died in this fight. It's a losing game. I don't see that you're going to make a difference so I might as well not get to know you. You won't be around for too much longer anyways." Cory stared into my eyes with a whole heartedly look of sadness in his face.

"Tell me about your dad, what was he like?" I asked Cory, I had to get through to this man somehow. "My dad was a fool, a good man nonetheless, but a fool. It never sat right with him that we had to stay in the caves while everyone else got to live happy and carefree up there. He grew angrier as the years passed. His brother was in the group of families that got banned. We would have been with him if it wasn't for Mom, she always had a way of keeping Dad grounded to reality. He was strong, brave and a hell of a lot better cook than I was. I was fifteen when they died and had to tend to myself. Cooking vittles was no easy task when you haven't done much but gone to school." Cory stared into the ground and was fiddling with his moccasin shoe lace. "How did they die, Cory?" I asked in a soft concerned whisper. "Well, Dad got fed up one day after I got real sick. He took off to Mason and demanded that something be done. He figured fine if we can't go outside here, why not move farther away. At least we would be outside there. He fought with mom for hours about it, and he promised he would be civil to Mason if he was granted the permission to talk to him. That was the last time I ever saw him. Mason held a town meeting a few days later and had said one of us had run out to the uppers to pick a fight. He didn't make it and it had caused more ruckus for us and for his disobedience our food was cut off for a while. Mason said he was tired of people taking it upon themselves to get things done. All it did was cause grief and I got sicker. Mom couldn't take it and she jumped...into the river outside our perimeter. It's quite a fall and there is no way she would have survived it. She was mad with grief though, I can't say I blame her." Cory stopped fidgeting with his shoe lace and just stared at Boe, lost in his memories.

"Look bud, your Dad was no fool. He was a patriot. Sometimes it takes those types of people to actually make things happen. In my world, we have many men like that. The problem is, when one man stands up for what is right it causes a small ruckus and gets shut down immediately. However, when many men stand up together for a common good...it causes change. It forces the people to look at what the problem is in the here and now, and do something about it. A revolution... An uprising if you will. It's the same back home, everyone wants to sit and complain about how things are being run. They want to nag about how bad things have gotten. But no one wants to join hands together and stand up and say enough is enough." Cory started to move his head upward and make eye contact with me. He didn't look shocked that I had said this. He actually almost seemed relieved. Like he was reluctant but forced to say these things about the man who raised him.

"My father...was another stubborn man. He had that same attitude. A patriot. He stood for what was right no matter the cost. He stood with a hundred men against unimaginable odds. He would travel the world all the time facing evil men, doing his best to right what was wronged. His theory was that someone had to stand on that wall to defend our nation. To defend our children...to defend me and my brothers. If he fought that fight away from home we wouldn't see bloodshed in our streets. We were free to go to school and do as we please. Along the way he got shot multiple times and barely escaped with his life. That man may be a fool, but who isn't Cory. That man is my ultimate hero and he always will be. If I could only live to be half the man he was, have half the bravery and courage that man possessed...I would be doing alright. If those men were fools bud, then I am quite the fool myself." Now it was my turn to look down at the ground, remembering Dad coming and going all the time. I was always angry too. Cory said nothing. "You know, I was always mad at him too. We never got along to say the least. The guy was always gone, and when he would come home...he was ruthless. It took me becoming a soldier myself to understand why he was the way he was. The things he had to go through to protect me. It changes people you know. Now, I can't believe I ever was mad at the man. Now, I won't ever get the chance to tell him that I actually love him and that I'm proud for all that he has done and sacrificed."

There was a good ten minute moment of reflection in the room when Boe had let out a sigh that broke the silence. "Will, you're not half bad you know. You have morals. That's good." Cory said with a sound of relief in his tone. "Well, you're not half bad yourself. They have a saying where I come from. Freedom isn't free. And how true is that saying. You and your people want freedom so bad but won't stand up together in unison for it. I may be able to get you on the surface, but rest assured the time will come when you're going to have to fight to stay there. Trust me, I don't enjoy killing. It's not really my thing. I would rather settle our differences over a drink. But the world doesn't work that way. And it takes men like your father, mine and myself to make things happen. One day it might take you, Cory" Cory stood up and stretched his arms into the air. Looking at him now in better light I would have to say that he is around his mid-twenties. "You know Will, when that day comes… it will be a happy one."

Cory and I exchanged stories of us growing up for another two hours before he stood up and called it a night. "You know, class starts tomorrow for the kids. If you would like to, you can join me. I usually head down there and check on all the villagers. It would do you some good to get out and stretch your legs a little bit. I don't feel like you are a major threat to our community. I feel like you would rather enjoy yourself. You might even be lucky enough to get some actual good chow instead of my own home cooking disaster. It would be nice for you to see what you're going to be fighting for." I nodded in reply and made him promise he would wake me up in time to leave. Cory walked out of the room, paused in front of Boe and scratched him behind his ears. Boe's heavy tail started smashing and beating the wall making all kinds of noise. "Dumb dog… cute though. " Cory whispered to him as he left the door with a smile on his face.

After petting Boe for another hour, he finally grew weary, jumped off the bed and took up his post underneath my bunk. Now I was utterly alone again. Seeing as no one wanted to hang out any more, I decided I would go and take my nap. It has been forever since I was able to sleep with no worries. I was pretty excited about the next day's little field trip. I felt like a kid getting ready for his first day of school, not knowing whether to be excited or fearful for the unknowing trials that lay ahead. I had been in my fair share of new schools and have somehow survived them all, so I decided to go with "excited," and call it a night.

CHAPTER TWELVE
"A town worth fighting for"

I walked out the door and half expected to feel the sunshine hitting my face, which would have been nice. But what I saw instead, pretty much broke my heart. We were definitely in a cave somewhere deep inside a mountain. It was a big cavern that had been hollowed out and made into a shabby village. Light poles were spaced out around the cavern in no specific order, adding a low glow of yellow ambiance to the already dark and gloomy environment. Somehow they had running power. Lights that were ran by some source that was way over my head to understand, no matter how many different ways they worded it. I just wasn't that smart.

Children ran the streets half-starved and dirty. They were my same height, it was amazing. Little kids that were four foot high, kicking a ball around the streets, Screaming and laughing. Their sounds were echoing off the walls, which magnified their joy. The mood in the streets was happy and carefree. In the midst of living in shambles, children always seem to find happiness. The ball made its way to me and hit me in the back of my calf. I reached down to pick it up and the streets became suddenly quite. I could feel the stares burning my skin at every possible angle. I picked up the ball and noticed it was very light in weight. I dropped it and kicked it to the nearest child, lighting a smile up on his face. The noise settled back in as the kids fought over who would have the ball next. Looked almost like soccer, just with more contact. Kids were elbowing other kids and tripping them to get control over the ball. It was very funny.

Everyone was so friendly here; it reminded me of back home in Kansas. Back where there were waves at every corner with bright and smiling faces. I couldn't understand how these people lived down here like this, while there was a whole world just feet above them, ready for the taking. Cory led the way into a small rock hut that could fit no more than twenty people inside. There were more of those small yellow orbs emitting light placed around the windows, letting light seep inside to what I assumed to be eager minds waiting to learn. If it was anything like my schools growing up, it would be full of bored minds eager to get out.

Once inside, there were perfectly carved chairs with kids no more than fifteen years old sitting in them. The chairs were sitting underneath a long table. Two tables altogether with ten kids per table. The room fell silent when I entered it. I guess I should get used to that by now. Cory and I nodded hello to the teacher who sat at the head of the class, and she carried on with her lecture. The teacher was a beautiful blonde with green eyes. She had a slender body and a nice set of legs. It's safe to say this was the most attractive woman I have seen since I have left Earth. She wore a dark skirt cut just above her knee's, with a top that showed a decent amount of cleavage. I sat, listening in on a few classes that were being held and learned of their history. I couldn't help but catch my eyes keep drifting up towards the instructor. Sometimes I hated being a man.

After a story that sounded something very familiar to our own revolutionary war story, I had to laugh to myself. This must have been what the British felt like after the American colonies smoked them up and sent them packing without a brown bag special. They sure didn't hide the shame in their defeat to the upper world people which the children knew as the 'sun people'. "Mr. Will, could you tell us of a conflict or war from your people?" Damn. She called me out. The slender blonde now stood four feet from me, glaring. I could tell now that she was about five foot five. Compared to the rest of the people I have seen here on this planet I would feel compelled to call her a midget or maybe even a smurf. But as far as my people go, she was just right. Her name was Ms. Ashley. And Ms. Ashley was a looker.

The only war that I knew a lot about was the civil war, so I figured I would spit some facts out about that. "Uhm, sure thing Misses, uhm... ya...misses Ashley." I cleared my throat obviously fumbling over my words, slightly embarrassed. I hadn't talked to a woman in I don't know how long. Clearly the class could tell I was being shy due to the snickers and giggles across the room. Miss Ashley stood there with a beautiful smile on her face and motioned for me to go on. "There was a revolutionary war just like the one you described a second ago, only our side won. The greatest conflict on our lands was that of the Civil War in the eighteen sixties. But even our history books are not accurate as to the true events of why the war was fought." I climbed to my feet and moved to the center of the classroom, maybe someone would finally listen to my redneck rant and be astonished. I doubt it, but I love to teach and talk, so I took advantage of the situation.

"In the mid 1800's the way of life was simple. We had states that had formed after the revolutionary war; we even had a President in charge of the whole country, except it wasn't a dictatorship like you guys kinda have going on right now... Long story short there is still a debate on the true reason of why the war started. You see, some history books said "slavery" was the reason the Civil War was fought. (I noticed a lot of blank stares from the people all throughout the room so I decided to elaborate a little.) Slavery is where one man forces another man to do his work for him with no pay. It was very cruel and inhumane. It's a very bad thing. The slaves would be chained up and beaten when they didn't obey. And most of them would be slaves for a long time, if not their entire life. Their own people enslaved them for money, sold them to the English and the Americans and it just floated down the line in such a manner. Slavery was a way of life for most people, most people with money, that is. It not only cost money to have a slave in your possession but it also cost money to feed and clothe them as well. Some would say this war was fought solely for the purpose of freeing the slaves, saying it was immoral."

I started to finally see the eager minds capture every word that I was speaking so I continued on. "What a lot of people don't know is the south was responsible for more than 70 percent of the income to the federal government. So when the South wanted to secede peacefully, the North could not afford the loss. There were other reasons as well, such as unfair taxes and laws. Regardless, the country separated, the

North versus the South. Once again, according to the books, the North wanted to abolish slavery, and the south wanted to keep them. So, supposedly this war raged for several years just over the right to own slaves." I let the room sink it in and could hear little side bars on how it was wrong, and they couldn't believe that slavery was ever allowed in the first place. After the disgusted jeers and snickers of the class room died down, I decided to move on. "What had really happened was this. The southerners were too poor to even own slaves, they were making just enough to get by. Roughly eighty-seven percent of all plantations in the south were owned by rich northerners. So yes, there were some southern owners, but the majority was definitely the Yankee's from up north. You see in the southern constitution…kind of like a piece of paper that explains all the new rules and guidelines…it clearly stated that the importation of slaves was hereby forbidden. Their plan was to let it die out naturally due to slave uprisings. They were scared the slaves were going to rise up like some others did in this place called Haiti and kill all the owners. "

"The war was fought over state's rights, the north wanted to come in and control how much the south could sell their crops for, and tax them like crazy. They were making federal laws and regulations that were preposterous and threatened the southern way of life, and the freedoms of every one south of the mason Dixon line! If the war was fought over slavery then why did the president of the Northern states make a letter stating that all slaves were to be freed immediately, and then have his own personal slave deliver the message. You do the math. I didn't make the story; I just tell it how it is. I think it stinks. Regardless, the north ended up winning in the long run, and low and behold my country is still taxed to death on anything that you could think of. You can sell milk for two dollars and sixty-seven cents a gallon but after taxes it ends up being close to four dollars. Doesn't seem right or fair, but that's how it is." I could tell I was in the middle of a rant and had lost the entire class; Cory was clearing his throat from behind me, signaling me to sit down and be done. I knew I had plenty more to say but I knew I wouldn't shut up on my rant any time soon, so I thought I would cut myself off and sit down. Miss Ashley looked at me with unblinking beautiful eyes; I couldn't help but have that feeling that she found me attractive as well. This was not good. Once again, I really hate being a man sometimes.

The kids in this class were skinny, bright eyed and smiling. They were nothing but knees and elbows mostly. Scrapes and bruises covered the palms of their hands and the caps on their knees. No doubt from running and falling on the hard ground of the cavern that they call home. There was laughter and smiling, jokes and horseplay. I felt like I had traveled back in time to my old high school. They looked almost sickly, if you stared at them just right. It was almost like I was at some special needs children hospital or something. They were sweet and kind, gentle and caring. They were kids. They were eager to learn and ready to listen. They made me miss my children back home.

A soldier has to find a fine line not to cross when it comes to family and war. If you think about them and miss them then your mind becomes conflicted with the best interest of the mission. If you learn to not miss them, time goes by faster and you are more effective at your job. I could tell their way of life living in these dark caves has taken a deathly toll on their health. It was definitely time to free these people. Someone had to or these beautiful children would surely die.

I followed Cory outside after class. There were rows of rock building lining both sides of what appeared to be a street. Laughter came out of some, cries from small children out of others. No one really seemed to mind me being there. I got waves and head nods on every corner. The sounds made from the kids playing in the streets echoed inside of my head as we made our way to the local bar, where we were to meet some of his friends. "Now, make sure to tell me if you are hurting too much to go on, and we will go home immediately," Cory told me in a very motherly voice. "I promise you that I am fine. I need to be out and about anyways, it is better for the healing," I assured him. We had reached the small tavern looking building about a half a block down on the left side of the street. The building was made of a mixture of rock and logs, puttied together with hardened mud and some sort of other chalky substance. The windows were like glass, with that same yellow light shining from within. It was strange, you couldn't actually see through them, and when you tapped on them, they were as hard as the side of the mountain itself.

We entered into the dimly lit room that revealed a group of four burly looking men in the back corner smoking on some sort of pipe. Man, what I wouldn't do for a hit off a smoke or a pinch of snuff... something with nicotine in it would be fantastic. The bar became immediately silent when I walked in. I felt that feeling of being uncomfortable immediately. These were not friendly stares. They must have been friends of the men I had killed upon my capture. I remember too well the feeling of an enemy being captured after blowing up a few of my fellow comrades. The government wanted to give him a fair trial and hold him accountable for his actions, and all we wanted was equal justice. Just kill the punk and all will be ok. That hatred sickening feeling that I have known over and over, I was sure they were feeling this same feeling towards me and it made me sick to my stomach.

Those men were someone's friends, lovers, and family, and I took their lives. What made my life worth living more than theirs? Hell, if it wasn't for me they would probably be sitting around this smoky bar right now, laughing and telling jokes. They would be playing with their kids in the street. "Look, guys...I did what I had to do and I am forever sorry. I was protecting myself. If this is going to be awkward or one of you guys are going to stab me while I'm in the bathroom, just let me know and I will leave now." My words broke the silence that hung over us like a stream of hot water on ice cubes, cracking with a more than loud enough whip. Everyone shook their heads no, and motioned for me to sit down.

The bar came back to life the instant that I sat down, and I felt like I had been accepted. All bad vibes and ill intentions seemed to fade away just as quickly as they had arrived. One of them passed the pipe my way and I took a puff, coughing instantly. This naturally triggered a group of laughter out of everyone at the table. I figured it would be tobacco but I was wrong. It tasted strangely similar to pot from back home. A slight spicy taste lingered in the roof of my mouth. It had been probably fifteen years since I have smoked pot, but I figured what the hell... might as well blend in and have a good time. It wasn't the taste or the strength of the smoke that startled me, it was like when you go to take a drink of water and it ends up being straight vodka. It just takes you completely off guard. A feeling of warmth waved over my entire body and singled in on my chest wound. Making it feel warm and tolerable. The pain I had been feeling for so long now just disappeared.

I took a couple of passes and handed the pipe to the guy on my left. They were making small talk about the weather upstairs, and what Sun people they had encountered. Battles won and battles lost. It was completely a normal smoke and joke session. There were six of them total, all built stronger than what I had seen floating around the cavern streets...much stronger. I didn't do much talking this time, I mostly observed. I don't know if this was due to the fact that I was completely worn out and exhausted from being up and around for the first time in a while...or simply because I was ridiculously high from the herb we had been smoking for the past hour.

It took me a little while to realize the herb even had an effect on me. Cory brought it to my attention that I had already ate five bowls of nuts and that he was going to order me some real food from the waitress. We all laughed together as I told him to go ahead because I could eat a horse right now. I could tell immediately that the waitress had a thing going on for Cory, and it appeared he felt the same way back. She was much taller than the slender teacher I had met at the school house. Dark black hair was messy on the top of an otherwise slimming face. Her eyes were blue and they would not leave Cory's. I finally realized that Cory just wanted a reason to talk to the lady. I had to laugh to myself about this, but couldn't bring myself to intervene in someone else's affairs. The waitress was in her mid-thirty's and even though she definitely looked old, she still had an attractive appeal about her. She wasn't exactly a looker, kind of chunky if you ask me, but something in her eyes made her seem desirable.

Her name was Anne and Anne was very loud and obnoxious. Apparently Cory liked this about her, probably because he was quite chunky himself and had a loud annoying laugh. I couldn't tell you what Cory see's in her, but I can tell he sees it. While I was trying to get rid of her and shut her up; Cory was enticing her to tell stories, and trying to make her laugh. I was growing weary of this woman and her ridiculous charades, but once Cory ordered me up some grub, it was on the table in less than four minutes flat. I was very impressed with the time standard here.

There was some sort of vegetable that was smothered in gravy, surrounded by mashed potatoes. I don't really do "vegetables," but one thing I will never turn down is mashed potatoes. Well, two things, a cookie and mashed potatoes. The smell was so strong it made the taste buds inside the corners of my mouth start a boxing match with my jaw muscles. It smelled delicious, so why not? I took the first bite and was immediately made aware of one fact; Cory couldn't cook to save his life. This was as big a difference as eating pot roast for dinner versus a bowl of noodles you can heat up in the microwave. This was the best thing I have eaten in over a year and there wasn't a shred of meat in it. Either way I was enjoying myself, my meal and my company. And everything thing about this evening, I found surprisingly humorous. A wooden fat goblet was slammed on the table in front of me and I was motioned to drink up. A foamy top covered the glass and it don't matter where you are in this galaxy, that could only be one thing, alcohol. A quick taste brought all my taste buds into action. A nice thick beer flavor flooded my body. It tasted so natural, so delicious I finished it with two big gulps and kindly asked for another. Everyone now was enjoying their drinks and getting louder and louder. More and more people came into the bar, singing and laughing. Two men started wrestling in the corner knocking over tables and chairs and breaking plates. I expected to see someone break it up, but everyone including Cory just cheered them on. Even Anne had her hand at the jeering.

After what had seemed like five hours in the bar, the hour had grown late and I was past worn out and ready to turn in for the night. I stood up, barely able to stand and Cory stabled me on my left. We said our goodbye's and headed for the door. I even got a few hand shakes out of it. These were definitely good people here. The best people I have actually met in a long time. I know it was against my better judgment but I started to feel like this place was a good place to call home. But home was with Stephanie, and Stephanie was not here. She needed me to get home and quick. Once we were outside the bar the temperature inside the cave had dropped at least twenty degree's. I could see the breath in front of my face mist up and spread upwards. I turned the corner to the house and ran smack dab into a tall lanky set of beady eyes staring at me almost hyperventilating.

"I hate to intrude on you like this but I am a huge fan of yours! My name is Chuck and I will do pretty much anything to learn at least half the things that you know. I have already been up in the sun many times; I've hunted and even killed before. It's too easy." The kid barely took a breath between sentences. I was tired and slightly annoyed so I brushed him off. "Go home kid, your parents are probably worried about you right now. I'll talk to you tomorrow, ok, bud?" Once inside of Cory's hut, he clued me in on this kid. "Chuck has no parents, Will. They were killed the same way my dad was. He has tried coming out on hunting trips with us, but he is too young and very head strong. He is loud and obnoxious, thinks he is a tough guy. He has been in trouble many times for going outside without the proper permissions. He's a trouble maker if you ask me." I sat and thought about it for a little while. "Sounds a lot like myself if you ask me." I said aloud to Cory.

Well, I was pretty bored during the day, and I have been called a trouble maker myself a time or two, so I decided to take him in. Worst case scenario I get annoyed and kick him out. It had to be better than this kid spending his time by himself getting into trouble, or worse because I am always getting into trouble. I walked back outside and saw him sulkily walking down the street, dragging his feet. He was about three blocks away so I shouted, "Chuck, get your butt back here, your bunking with me now!" I walked back inside and told Cory to go set up a sleeping pallet in my room with Boe. "Will, I don't know about all this, this kid is like a leach. Once he latches on there is no shaking him," Cory told me, trying hard to talk to me out of it. "Just do as I say and trust me for once," I laughed.

Chuck had made his way into the bedroom huffing and puffing from his recent sprint. I showed him his pallet and he was like a brand new puppy, looking at everything top to bottom. "Shut up and go to sleep, kid. In the morning I am going to train you to be the toughest kid in these caves. You're going to be my right hand man." Chuck reluctantly began to lie down on his quickly made pallet. With the lights off, I could hear him breathing. I could hear all the questions he wanted to ask in his quick rapid breaths. "Mr. Do you like..." I immediately cut him off. "Shut up Chuck."

The room got quiet again. I was starting to feel the effects of the herb kicking in and taking my pain away. Maybe I could finally get a decent night of sleep. I started to see my wife's beautiful face riding behind me on my motorcycle. Hair tied back in a ponytail, secured with a bandana. She was so sexy. "Mister, I was just wondering real quick..." Chucks words blasted the picture of my wife's face straight out of my head. "Damn it kid, I swear you are about to sleep outside if you say another word. One more word and I'm going to choke you out." Boe let out an annoyed groan from his hidden cave underneath my bed and the room finally fell silent. Now where was I? Ah yes, beautiful blonde ponytail holding onto me tight on the back of my bike. Good dreams.

CHAPTER THIRTEEN
"Making plans"

The next morning came earlier than I had hoped. I woke up to Chuck setting a plate of hot food on my chest, burning my chest hairs straight to the skin. "What the hell dude, give a guy some warning or something!" I barked. Chuck gave me his apologies and I had to calm myself. I realize that he is just trying to impress me, and being rude wasn't really helping at all. I know he wanted to prove himself useful, and what he really was trying to do was to get chosen for this upcoming mission. The pain in my chest was significantly better. I felt under my shirt and felt scabs already forming a rough lining on top of my wound. This was impossible; I shouldn't be at this stage for another couple of weeks.

I can't even begin to describe what this food might be, it looks utterly disgusting. hesitantly I start to eat what he has given me. Amazingly enough, whatever it is, I found it to be very flavorful and hit the spot for breakfast. "This is pretty good, Chuck. I might have use for you after all. So what can you do besides cook a good meal entirely too early in the morning?" Chuck took a deep breath and started to answer in a very eager excited tone that was entirely too chipper this early in the morning. "I can shoot an arrow straighter than anyone I know, and I know a lot of people. I can hunt anything that moves, skin it, clean it and cook it. I know every foot path from here to the nearest five villages. I am quiet and sneaky..." I had to cut in. "I don't know about quiet." I laughed, but he didn't even act like it fazed him, he just continued on his 'I'm so awesome' rant... "I have killed over a dozen men, only those that threatened me of course. I am a great learner, I excelled way over my classmates... when I was in school, and I catch on very quickly. I can draw really well. As a matter of fact, I have made my own maps for you, in case I ever had the honor of meeting you, which I obviously did." I sat and thought to myself that this kid might actually be an asset to the mission.

I am glad that he barged in and threw himself at me, instead of me having to hunt someone down with his capabilities. Already better than little Gerald. "Well, Chuck, first off, I want you to go home and get me those maps. Secondly, I would like for you to bring me every weapon that you have, and materials to build more. You know like arrows, spears, knives and so forth. We need to make a weapons cache that will be big enough to support what we have going on here. I'm not going to meet the rest of the team for another two weeks, but I think I want you to lead my men out there on a few scouting parties. That is if you can handle it. I will need to expand what we know a little bit. The more that you do… the less that I have to do. Are you tracking?" In a flash Chuck was out the door, leaving Boe and I in silence. Nice complete silence. Of course I went to back to bed. I needed a power nap, I can't quite recoup from a long night like I used to. I was getting old after all.

The knock on my door made me jump, yet again. Chuck came rushing in with his arms full of weapons, some elementary and others pretty advanced. He had somehow came up with a crude model of a cross bow, and I liked it. Apparently it was still too early for Boe because he snuck out the door, to go sleep in the kitchen no doubt. Lucky dog. The room was quiet and I was sure that Chuck was looking for some sort of compliment for all of his work. I know I would have wanted one. Instead, I left him hanging, as I inspected everything that he had laid out. They were in great shape. If I hadn't known any better, they were brand new. But if you looked close enough you could see the time that he took to maintain them. This kid had all the makings of a good soldier. There were plenty of good long knives, throwing knives, machetes and axes. Over to the left were two cross bows, a regular bow, and over two hundred arrows. The arrows were grouped by tens though, every head being different. He went on to explain to me that half of the arrows had poison tips that would paralyze his prey for over thirty minutes. A group of twenty arrows in the back were deadly to the touch. A lethal arrow…I like it.

There were bundles of sticks and a bucket full of stones just the right size to make heads out of. What I was looking most forward to was the maps which he had laid out on my bed. They were small, but very well defined. Every creek bed, which I call a "waddy," were drawn out perfectly and labeled with their depth and width. It appeared that this kid had traveled roughly twenty miles around the caverns in all directions. "Well, I have to say, I am deeply impressed with what you have here… and you have appeared to motivate me on some level, so, let's get to work. About how long does it take you to make a cross bow?" I ask him, eager to get up and start doing something productive. Chuck, who was obviously pleased with himself, answered immediately, "Two hours tops." The first thing that crossed my mind was yeah, right. I said, "Be realistic, man. I don't want anything faulty. Good dependable weaponry is all I need, we have time." Chuck dropped his head and muttered out what I am pretty sure sounded like, "a day." "That sounds better. Let's slow it down and make it two days. Get started, because I want two more."

Chuck left the room to go build my weapons and I grabbed up the maps to study. It looks like there are only five small towns within close proximity to the caves. What I would like to know, is exactly how big of an area I am working with here. Are we on a continent? Are we on an island or something? The shuttle that we came in on was blacked out so we couldn't see anything on the entrance, and we hardly left the base when we actually got here. When we did leave, we didn't go farther than five miles out. I had no idea of what a bird's eye view of this land was, but I needed to find out. It was detrimental to what I had to do. It was one thing to move a group of men on foot for about 100 miles and quite another to move them 1,000 miles.

I looked over the maps one more time. If we took the passage way out this way to the left…we would only hit one town, which we could definitely skirt. I needed to know where this man lived, and how far it was to get there. Without this knowledge I was going nowhere, and could not prepare properly. There is sure to be scouts or bases around. Something that lets the sun people know when these guys come out of the caves.

I walked out of the room and saw Boe still being lazy on the kitchen floor. I poked my head around the corner to find Cory mixing something together in his living room. "You know bud, you should really find a girl or something, leave the house, go and smell the musty air of your cave. Do something crazy and get a life." We both laughed for a minute. "Well Will, since you had your new friend I figured I would work on a new concoction for your chest wound. The smoke from the tavern is a risky smoke; some people react differently to it and don't like the effects. You are healing very nicely and I think with this put into the mix you should be up and running very shortly. The sooner you are up and running the sooner that you can go home." I couldn't argue with that, so I proceeded to pound him with all the questions I had built up in mind.

"Ok, here we go. One, where does this guy Q live? I want to know how far we are talking about. Half a day walk? Are we talking a week's worth of traveling? A month maybe? Give me something here. I need to know exactly how far I am expected to go, because that will have a great effect on how many people I can bring, and what kind of training we need to get done before we set out."

Cory sat and thought for a while, for too long if you ask me. From personal experience, when someone takes this long to answer a question, it usually means the answer that eventually follows is pulled straight up from the middle of nowhere. They just make crap up. "If you don't know man, just let me know that you don't know, and let's find someone who does know," I butted into his deep concentrating thinking.

"No, Will, it's not that. I have never been there myself, but I'm trying to remember how far my dad said it was. He used to tell me stories about it. I want to say, it's about a good three day hike from here. The terrain is pretty rough from what I have been told, so lots of breaks make up most of the time span." I sat down on the couch and started contemplating my game plan. I could push these guys to make it there in two days, which really isn't that bad. We would move as a small element. I might only take ten of us, maybe twelve. Being small, agile and undetectable was definitely a must in this case. If we were compromised at all, we would all be dead.

From what I could figure, the reason in the size difference between the two nations, which were about to stand toe to toe with one another, was due mostly to the lack of protein in their diets. They didn't get any of the meat that roamed the open plains above. There must have been something inside of the meat that beefs you up, sort of like a steroid of some type. I noticed most of the hunters, and even Chuck, were built much stronger and sturdier than their underground counterparts. I also think that exposure to the multiple suns has a bit to do with it as well. I am not a scientist, but it makes sense that it has to have some sort of effect on a person's body and physique. I have even seen changes in myself since I have been here. I have grown a few inches and gained a good twenty pounds in muscle mass.

I need a hunting party and I need them to eat the hell out of some meat. Sounds like a good mission for Chuck. I had sent Cory into town with a message for Gerald to come and see me immediately, and to also hunt down Chuck. I needed to get started as soon as possible. Chuck came in huffing and puffing and plopped himself into the uncomfortable couch-like seat I was sitting on in the living room. "Well kid, are you going to make it? You dying on me or what? Looks like you're a little out of shape," I joked. I had to speak up due to his ragged breathing. "Rule number one kid. When you're tired, don't show it. If the enemy finds out you are weak, you're dead." Chuck's cheeks reddened at his embarrassment, and he was fighting to keep his breath low and quiet. "Here is the deal, Chuck. I need meat and lots of it. Go find a couple of buddies that you can trust, and bring back as much good meat as you can. I don't want it to spoil, so don't take forever. I am going to teach you how to smoke it, and make it last much longer. The deal is, the more meat you people eat, the stronger you will become. We don't have much longer until we are leaving. You guys are going to need your strength." Just as quickly as Chuck appeared, he disappeared out the door. I could tell he was excited to leave the cave, and for that I was grateful. I needed someone who liked an adventure as much as I did.

All was silent in the house. I drew up a blueprint to make a dehydrator for the meat. I really hadn't done this in mass before, but the concept should be the same. Pretty much smoke them out, and then hang them to dry, and bam! We are done. I am hoping it will be just that simple. To be honest, I am not what you would call a "builder." I would describe myself more as having a friend that can build, and I just "hang out, supply the beer and grill for everyone" type of guy. That was more of my specialty. I could grill all day long out here, but it does me no good if I can't save the meat afterwards. There was no way to keep the meat from going bad after a few days out in the woods, and then it smells and the bugs get to you, it's a lose-lose situation.

The blueprints took me about half the day to draw up, and then I had the little problem of locating the right supplies. So of course, I sent for Cory to go pick them up. Nothing too crazy, I needed mainly wood. I could chop it and trim it by myself. I was feeling much better now, and I really hate sitting on my butt and doing absolutely nothing. A few days of doing nothing can be quite awesome from time to time, but a few weeks of doing nothing could kill a man, figuratively speaking, of course.

CHAPTER FOURTEEN
"Moral Cross roads"

Over the next few days, Cory and I had built an amazing smoker if I do say so myself. We had racks that were long enough to dry out an entire elk if we wanted to. This should definitely suffice in feeding my troops for the time that we will be gone. I'm estimating that it will take on average, about one day to dry out and prepare each animal. What day we can actually leave this place will be dependent upon on exactly how many animals Chuck is able attain on his hunt.

Chuck drug himself, three friends and four sleds full of dead animals into the opening of the cave on the fourth day and they were all smiles. Apparently they had a good time, which is good, because happy troops are good troops. Chuck had three wild hogs that had to have weighed at least 600 pounds each. A good size buck was on the fourth sled. Not bad for a few days hunting trip. It is important to drain the blood so the meat doesn't spoil, I am glad he knew this already.

Out of the three men that Chuck had brought with him, there wasn't a single one of them that weighed less than 180 pounds of solid muscle. I could tell these were most definitely the trouble makers of the town...exactly who I wanted with me. So I figure I will recruit these guys. If they are always into trouble then they won't have any problems getting into "more" trouble with me. I need team members who will not hesitate to pull the trigger or go out on mission when told at the last second.

"Nicely done, Chuck, I said proudly. I need you to drag the meat around to the back of the house, because we're going to skin these guys and start smoking 'em. When the food is done, we are rolling out the gate brother, so get your rest and say your goodbyes. It's going to be us four, plus some nerdy guy that Mason has demanded that I let tag along for the ride. If he even shows back up that is. I doubt they are going to send anybody worth anything, so you boys will suffice. So go home, relax and get ready. We leave in the morning." From the looks on all their faces, it seemed that I had just told them they won the lottery.

I would much rather go out with the six of us, than go out with a team of twenty five, with twenty four complete rookies. The chances of survival and mission accomplishment were growing greater by the minute. I was so excited to go do this, I could hardly contain myself. I have to admit, the break has been nice, but I am beginning to grow quite stir crazy. I can't sit in one spot for too long, or I come up with stupid things to do. I know we weren't scheduled to leave for another week or so, but I was ready to go now.

If I operate with a six man team, I can cut the travel time completely in half, I will be able to maneuver my men completely concealed and hopefully bring most of them home, which brings me home. I personally can't wait to get home. I bet my wife is waiting up on me right now, listening to every car pass by the window, hoping one will be me. All four of the boys just stood there and posted up by the smoker as I prepared the meat to be hanged. "I thought I said to go home to your families. This is kind of a big deal I can't promise you that you will all make it back." I told them. Chuck spoke up, clearly the leader of the group. "We are our family, and apparently now you." "Well, in that case…take a seat and I will tell us some stories."

"I remember one mission that went bad in Russia. We went in as a small security detail for a prime minister. The prime minister really pissed off a bunch of Russians, and for some reason we had mobs of people coming after us. I barely escaped with my life, lost all of my men, with one of them being my best friend. Of course the minister himself had his own escape plan…big enough for himself. I had promised my wife, like I do ever time, that I would make it home, that there would be nothing that would keep us apart. I always tell her even if we are worlds away, I will always come home. Of course I had no idea at the time that I would be quite literally, worlds away… enough about me why don't ya'll tell me about yourselves." I'm sure they didn't just want to hear about me. "No Will, you started this, now you have to finish it." Cory chimed in as he showed up with more chairs and huge buckets of beer for the team. The boy's eyes lit up and we all filled our cups.

"So there I was, hauling ass through the forest of Russia looking for any way to get my hands on a boat. I would have used a plane; however, I have learned that the government can track and shoot down planes a lot easier than boats. Boats can be disguised. I hitched a ride with a group of fisherman headed for deeper waters and bigger fish. It took me seven months of traveling from boat to boat, cargo ships to connex's. Eventually I hit the shores of Mexico, a small third world country just south of my country, and barely skipped passed the Federali's searching the cargo. Once in Mexico, I figured it would be super easy to jump the border and head home to Oklahoma. Unfortunately, I had no papers on me whatsoever, which is kind of a rule in my line of work when we go outside the wire. No identification on your person at all. So yea, you hear of Mexicans jumping the border all the time, kids and all. They live in America forever, happy and free. Well, that is until they get caught and deported back home, then they just jump it again. It's a continuous cycle that can never be broken. So just how hard could that be, if kids can do it all the time then I should be able to with ease right?" I ask my new team. I notice they had all taken seats around the fire box and were listening intently.

"Super hard, in case you're actually wondering," I answered. "I made it up to a town right near the border with a name that I couldn't pronounce at all. There was not one single break in the wire and I really didn't care if I was caught on the American side. I could always talk myself out of that one. I figured I would just steal a car and bust through the fence, ditch the car at the first town in Texas and be home in a few short hours. I had already taken on a few rounds of ammo through the windshield before I even made it through the fence. It didn't help that the car I stole was an old Ford Pinto. In my defense, it was the only car around at the time. This baby was lime green, had shag carpet and red tassels hanging off the head liner. It was a classic piece of shit. It back fired every time you would hit the gas, so being inconspicuous was definitely not in the realm of reality for this car." I realized at this point, no one here knew what a "car" was, but it was a good story, so I continued.

"I had to run over three Federali's before I ever made it to the fence. To my surprise, this piece of shit car couldn't even make it through the fence! I had been traveling for months, so I was in no shape to run the few miles that lay in the valley between the first town in America and halfway under a fence where I currently resided. I had that old Pinto floored and smoke poured from the tail pipe, and a blazing white thick fog just billowed out from all angles under this car. I could smell the rubber finally starting to catch the surface on the ground long enough to give that good rubber burning smell the chance to sting your nostrils. I think I was moving maybe two inches every ten seconds under the fence... barely creeping through, but I was moving none the less. At the rate I was going, I would be out and on solid ground in roughly thirty seconds." I could feel the excitement building up around the fire so I paused for effect taking a big swig off my cup.

"I remember looking back through the back glass and seeing tons of those Mexican cops running at me full speed, just bursting rounds into the back of my newly acquired vehicle. I had barely slipped out of the fence when they reached my bumper. I was all the way in the floor board, using my hand to punch down that heavy foot pedal to the floor, just trying not to get shot. I barely got that old jalopy two miles from the nearest town before the motor blew. I figured I would get out on foot and hoof it in. I could hear the helicopters and the four wheelers closing down on me. I desperately needed to be in town when they caught me, preferably at the police station. That way, those renegade border patrol punks don't try and beat the hell out of me and just throw me back over the fence." Everyone was laughing and I could tell Cory was trying to visualize the scene I was painting.

"I don't think I ever ran that fast in my life. Those border patrol guys were just complete gung hoe idiots. They were notorious for always catching the good guy on accident and never catching the bad guy, besides the fact that they are all crooked as hell. I lucked out that time. The Sherriff's office was right on the first block inside the town. The Border Junkies were no more than two hundred meters behind me when

I had kicked the door open and stated screaming who I was at the top of my lungs. I started screaming 'I'm a US citizen! I'm a Citizen! Of course everyone thought me to be a lunatic, which I had already expected. I was arrested and put into an interrogation room." Everyone laughed at this part which fueled me to keep going with the story.

"Once I was entered in the system, it didn't take but ten minutes tops before the FBI showed up to debrief me, and escort me home. Apparently they had already given my wife a flag stating that I had died for my country. They fed her the whole line, hook and sinker. However, my wife didn't buy it, because my ring was not there." I paused for effect showing them my wedding ring on my dog tags that were tied to my belt loop and tucked nicely into my pocket.

"I have always lived off of the rule that if my ring ain't given to her, then I ain't really dead, and she needs to hold on a little longer 'cause I was on my way home, somehow." The group fell silent and my story was over. The boys started talking to themselves about the hunting trip and how awesome Chuck's new crossbow was.

I keep trying to fight off the memories of my wife. Amazing memories and my beautiful wife aside, I have a mission to do. The time was drawing near, and I need to prepare. We had a large enough dehydration stack to dry everything at once, so we will be leaving tomorrow morning. The boys all migrated into the living room stumbling over everything and in high spirits. They fell asleep immediately. I'm sure they were exhausted.

I need to find this Jerold kid, wherever he was. He needed to come prepare for the trip. I had Cory make bags for everybody while they slept; he had only made ten, which works, because now I only need six. I walked back through the house and yelled for Cory to come to my room to help me pack. When he showed up he looked very nervous. "What's the dealio, there cheerio? Why the scared look?" I asked him, trying to input a little humor into the equation. My words didn't lighten him up, probably because he didn't know exactly what a "cheerio" was.

"Will, I overheard you saying that you were leaving in the morning. I have to admit I am worried about you leaving this soon, as you are not all the way healed up. You know, you don't even have to do this. The community likes you and I think you fit in quite nicely here. You can even work the security detail and protect the people..." Cory trailed off while looking over at Boe, who hadn't really left the room in like six hours. What a lazy mutt.

"Cory, number one, stop being such a girl about this, I don't belong here. I have a family back home, and they expected me home freaking ages ago. I appreciate the hospitality and I really do like it here. It is nice and peaceful, aside from the fact that there is no sun...ever. That's a pretty big downer for me, I won't lie." Cory wouldn't answer me he just had that look. It was actually more of a look like he had a secret he really wanted to tell, but was worried about getting in trouble. This guy reminded me of a huge kid. I almost felt like he was my little brother. He was dumb as a box of rocks when it came to common sense and had a horrible laugh. But he always came through for me and took care of me when I needed it the most. That was the quality of a great friend.

"Will, I need to tell you something." "Damn it Cory, I knew it, they're going to kill me anyways aren't they. They don't have a fuel source for me; I'm getting screwed in this thing ain't I?" I cut in furiously. I have a bad habit of losing my temper, especially when I am getting the raw end of the stick.

"No, Will, I am going to be honest with you here ok, so don't be mad at me. While you were asleep, I stole your map that had directions back to the ship that you made. We sent a team of guys back there to bring it here. They are already back. Word got back today that they know what can fuel it enough for roughly nine months' worth of traveling, according to Mason. We have equipment deeper in the cave that we keep hidden that runs off a liquid that has been made. We use them for emergency purposes only, or when we build things. The smell that comes from them when they are running can kill people, so we don't ever use them. But we do have a lot of the liquid to power them." Cory paused briefly then continued.

" I can sneak you deeper into the caves and you can just leave. All you have to do is wait to leave for another few weeks, and I will let you know when it is ready. You don't have to do this at all, you have done enough. We can survive on our own down here; we have been doing it for years. Worst case scenario, I have a brother that lives deep inside the caves. He has a bunch of friends and they are the type of people not to be messed with. They stay hidden at all times, they hate everyone. They can help you get to your ship, though." Cory got quiet and I had nothing to say.

I wasn't exactly mad. I mean, I don't like people sneaking through my stuff at night while I am sleeping, and Boe should have bit him in the process. So really, this is Boe's fault. He should have known better. "Cory, I appreciate your honesty, and it's good to know your people came through in the end. I was for sure I was getting screwed there for a minute. But you guys kept up your end, now I need to keep up mind. I promised to free your people and that is what I am going to do. That is the least I can do for you. If you don't mind, I am tired and need some sleep." Cory apologized and left the room.

There was so much to contemplate. I could just leave, that would be the smartest thing to do. I can play the "I'm hurt" card for a little while, and then sneak off in the ship. Once it is fueled and I was in the air, there would be no stopping me. They may have some horses or something, but they don't have anything to chase me in and nothing to shoot me down in once I launch. But even if it fuels my ship, we built this ship ourselves…how do I know this thing is even going to make it out of the atmosphere and this fuel is sufficient enough to power it. It is definitely risky, but I would rather die trying to get home to my family than not try at all.

I lay down in my bed and Boe jumped up and snuggled in next to my chest. "Yea, thanks for letting people steal from us, you little bastard," I whispered in his ear, as I played with the short tussle of hair that had matted up on top of his head. "We could be home in a few weeks definitely man, what do you think about that?" Boe's tail was wagging and slapping the side of my leg. This dog's tail was probably the most violent thing on him; it would break a door down if he was happy enough. I know Boe wanted to go home with me, and I wanted take him.

If we took this mission there was a big chance that we wouldn't succeed and no one would be going home at all. But, if I just left these people in the night and flew home, I would be home with my family in a matter of months. I'm not saying that I have never done a crooked thing before or that I haven't screwed anyone over to get a better deal for myself. But hey, a man has to do what a man has to do sometimes, right? And my wife, my kids, family and friends are just waiting on me to get home. This was very tempting. A moral cross roads. I really hate being in these shoes.

I could hear the boys tending to the meat in the back of the house. Apparently they couldn't sleep for very long. They had the pre-mission jitters. They wouldn't sleep a wink tonight guaranteed. At least we would have some meat to eat for the next few weeks. I don't know how I would break it to them that I have changed my mind. These guys look up to me, especially Chuck. Lying in my bed and listening to them cutting up outside reminded me of camping back home. I would usually have too much to drink and pass out in my tent, listening to the sound of the lake and the campfire. The last survivors of the party could be heard still laughing around the fire.

A quick image of my dad flashed through my head. That man was a true hero. He was shot multiple times back in the Iraqi Freedom campaign. That man would always hold up to his word. I couldn't imagine if he would be disappointed in me leaving these people with my word being shattered to shreds. Or maybe he would give me the 'you had to do what you had to do' speech I sometimes get. Sleep overtook me and I faded away into wonderful dreams of motorcycle rides and amazing breath taking memories of my wife. I was trying to think of anything but the choice I had to make when I woke up. It would definitely be easier for me to just disappear into the night. Maybe I could just let chuck and his boys do the mission. They were more than capable. They seemed like a pretty smart lot.

CHAPTER FIFTEEN
"I smell a rat"

Boe woke me up quite early in the morning; I could tell it was early because the room was ice cold and humid. I could hear Cory's muffled voice through the walls, trying to break it to the boys that I was still hurting, and the trip was going to have to be postponed. I got up out of bed and started to walk toward the back door. Boe was right next to me, except he looked different. He looked like that dog I had found in the woods a while back. That cautious stance, the Mohawk standing up on his back indicating that he was ready for an adventure. He stared at me judging me. "Well, what would you have me do man?" I whispered to Boe as I leaned down to scratch him behind his ears. Boe stood up and walked over to my pack and sat. "I see you are for staying around and doing the right thing huh…"

I opened up the door and walked out towards the group by the fire pit. Everyone fell silent as I approached. Cory looked sad again, but I could see the glint of hope in his eyes. He was hoping and praying that I would apologize for not feeling better but would promise we would go out soon. Jerold was even there, in all his glory. What little glory there was of him that is. That kid is probably going to get killed the second we leave the cave, and probably by seeing the sunlight. "Boys....I'm going to need some help pulling these packs out of the room, we leave in thirty minutes."

I turned to leave, and could feel the excitement rise up in everyone, including myself. Boe was back to his normal self. I couldn't leave these people to die down here; it wasn't right on any level. Everyone deserves freedom. Jerold was the first person in my room, throwing an elaborately made map on my bed. I'll give him this; the kid can certainly draw a map. "Will, the trip will take roughly two weeks on foot. Since you are only taking us five. I calculate that we could make it in less than one week. As long as we stop here and here and here and here..." Jerold was pointing to black dots that had been drawn all over the map along the route.

"I get it Jerold, good job. We stop at the marked spots for breaks and chow. Tell me more about where we are after this point up here." I pointed to a section of the map just before a giant x. "What are we expecting, and are they going to be expecting us?" Jerold pulled his pants up a little higher to his belly button, if that was at all possible, and continued.

"Well, Q is located in this town, Bella Dry Vista. He travels with no less than five personal guards. He lives in this corner of the town near the wood line. The best time to get him with as small of an entourage as possible will be early morning or late night. According to the tradition, once he is dead, you should be able to walk right up there and take charge. He does, however, command a larger group of people that fight for him, estimated to be around sixty to one hundred people. And that's not counting his small ruthless hunting parties that he frequently sends out. You have killed some of them, so we haven't been able to keep an accurate count of them in the past few months. At one time there was over thirty groups of three to four man teams that would go out." You could tell where Jerold had pointed out on the map where he believed the hunting parties to be located.

I noticed water surrounding the land mass that Jerold had been drawing on and he must have picked up on the question I was about to ask. "We live on an island, as you call it. There is water surrounding us on all sides, and we are here (he pointed to an X on the map at the bottom, next to a mountain and a lake) and we are going here (Another x in the middle of the map, surrounded by trees)." This was a very smart kid, and it looked like they had been doing surveillance for a while on this guy. The entire route was highlighted, with detailed rest stops, and how long we should spend at every rest stop. The island looks to be about the size of Texas.

"Ok, we are using everything but your route and your rest stops. I will determine those, if your plans have somehow been compromised at all, those are all perfect ways and routes to die on. You better put on your running shoes kid...we're getting there in less than three days. So, with that said, we are leaving. Go say good bye to your mom or whatever and meet me out in front in like ten minutes. And we are not stopping for any potty breaks for a while, so you better go while you are here," I told Jerold in an almost too rude of a tone. I am pretty sure I hurt his feelings. The fact remains though. I don't know who gave him this route, but I am coming up with my own route. I just need a start and an end point, that's it. It is safer and muck quicker that way. There was just something about this kid and this map that made me uneasy. Mason had not been helpful at all during the preparations of this trip. That in itself wasn't normal.

Everyone was outside in less than ten minutes, including Mason, who was super mad that I was only taking a small group instead of a force. He had twenty shady looking men behind him. "Mason, I make the rules and you follow them ok? This is what I am going to do, and then we will be home. Expect us back in roughly two weeks. Tell your boys to go to the tavern and have a drink on me, Anne makes a pretty mean dinner so they can just relax until we get back. The fuel needs to be ready at that point. I expect to be going home the second I return."

My group of six walked proudly through the corridors of the cave as everyone in the village rushed out screaming and cheering us on. The moment was a proud one, I won't deny it. Kids were on shoulders waving their little hands and smiling faces with rosy red cheeks. These children deserved freedom and I was going to be the man to give it to them. Boe was hot on my heels and I could hear his breathing becoming louder as we reached the mouth of the cave. I noticed Miss Ashley from the other day poking her head around the corner, staring. She ran up to me and gave me a kiss on the cheek. "Thank you so much for this, we will forever be in your debt." "Look, Miss..." She interrupted me still entirely too close to my face. "You can call me Ash." She said while blushing. "I know your married and your heart is with her, she is a lucky woman and I hope she knows that." Our eyes locked and I felt myself blush. I have never cheated on my wife and I wasn't about to start. It hasn't happened yet, and it won't be happening any time soon. But there was something about her eyes that made me look one last time. It gave my heart a flutter just looking at her. I smiled and then turned my head back towards the path. I have to admit it made me feel good.

The morning air was crisp to the touch and cold to the lungs. However, the suns had already made their appearance in the morning sky, hanging just above the brim of the lake. It was beautiful. We all stood and watched as Gerald looked at the lake and suns for the first time in his life. A tear formed up underneath his left eye, and I could tell he was trying to hold it in. I am sure this would be the same reaction from most of the people below us who have never gazed at a beautiful sunrise before. The look on Gerald's face made everything worth it. Because of me he has been able to receive this gift. What he doesn't know is he is going to have to fight with his life on the line in order to keep it. This did bring up a good point; he has never been out here, so how was his maps so detailed? Maybe we should check out his first point for good measure. If it's compromised then something is definitely amiss.

We walked for a good thirty minutes in a staggered out v formation. Boe had the lead a good ten meters in front of the rest of us. He was ready and vigilant and I trusted him. He was as good a point man as any if you ask me. We reached the bowling ball rock which is where Gerald had pointed out was our first rest stop. I went to the left of it and wanted to get a little closer for a look. The map showed we would come in from the south, so coming in from the east would be unexpected. This would give me a good idea if anyone else knew we were coming. If they had gotten wind we were out for blood, this is where a party would be waiting on us to try and change our minds. At least that's what I would do. Demoralize my enemy right out the gate and make them go home. Also, if someone was waiting on us here, that meant that a certain someone could not be trusted. That would mean Gerald was a rat. If there is one thing that I hate, it's a rat.

Boe tensed up and I could tell he caught the scent of a hunting party and I had caught the scent of a rat. I knew it was too perfect, the routes all planned and highlighted. The rest stops pin pointed. Something was amiss here, and when I finish with the punks down at the bottom of the bowling ball, I will deal with Gerald. All signs are pointing to that kid right now and it's not going to be pretty.

"Gerald, bunker down right here...ok bud. Chuck and I will be right back." I instructed the rat as I motioned for Chuck to head over my way. I took him up to the edge of the bluff and we looked down amongst the rocks and saw our enemy, all six of them. Once again, huge guys awaited my entrance. "Chuck, take your cross bow and circle around, without being seen ok. Boe will go in first and that will be your signal. When he takes his first guy I want you to send two dudes to the grave from your angle and rush in and finish them by hand, got it? I want to send a damn message to anyone who is watching that we will not surrender. I am for real here. If you bitch out on me, I will kill you myself I swear it. I need every ruthless bone of your body to come out right now. Remember slow is smooth and smooth is fast. When you get to the hand to hand part, make it bloody."

Chuck looked at me with a fire in his eyes. "Too easy Will. Two arrows, two guys, kill shots. I go in and we finish the rest by hand and be brutal. What are you waiting on, let's roll!" Chuck whispered to me in a loud excited whisper. I could tell this is what he had been waiting on for a long time. A chance to do some damage and this was his time to shine.

Chuck took off at sprint and circled around to the right side of the rock. What the party at the bottom of the hill didn't realize, is you always have to use your terrain to your advantage, and right now, they were fish in a barrel. I motioned for the other members of my team to come to me. "Ok boys, here's the deal, Chuck is going to send in two arrows, take down two guys and move in to kill the rest by hand. I want you two to go in through the middle, ok? I want you to break these men in half. And you...wait here with Gerald; don't like that bastard out of your sight till I get back. I promise you will have time to go down there and do some dirty. I just need to get this party started. I will deal with him when we are done here. Move out." With military precision my troops moved out, just as eager and excited as Chuck.

Once lined up in my position, I glanced around at the heads of the rocks on the corners. Everyone was in place, and they were itching for a fight. The group at the bottom of the hill looked like they were getting ready to pack up and take their positions to attack us. I put an arrow in the notch and drew back my bow, steady now. The pain in my Chest started to slowly throb. "Now is not the time to be in pain, Will," I told myself. My arrow left with a soft *thwak* and melted right into the middle of the leader's head knocking him from his feet and sending him teen feet back landing on his face. Everyone at the bottom looked stunned and surprised as the big oaf did a complete backflip and laid there no longer moving.

Not even two seconds had elapsed when three more arrows began flying into the center of the arena, each arrow sinking right where it was intended. There were only three of them left so I sent Boe in, who obliged without regret. That dog wanted blood as much as I did. Once Boe let out a bark both of my soldiers stormed the valley. I sat and watched as my herd of dominions did what they did best, they killed. I went back and grabbed Jerold by the scruff on the back of his head, dragging him over where he could get a better look. The boy that was watching Gerald took off to catch up with the rest of the team. They wanted this. "Will, you're hurting me, what did I do!? I don't understand!" The rat cried and moaned as I drug him to the edge of the cliff, where he would have a first class view of the slaughter.

I reached around and put Jerold into a sleeper hold, but waited to apply the pressure. I wanted him to feel helpless and terrified as he watched his counterparts get slaughtered with no mercy. I cinched tighter and tighter around his neck letting him feel the darkness fade in then back to reality. He saw the whole scene. I wanted him to know I was going to do the same to him, and there was nothing he could do about it.

Chuck ran up on the first man, who was easily three times his size. While jumping off a rock he launched himself at least six feet in the air, thrusting his knife into the side of the oaf's neck, which sent the big man to his knees. He let out a huge blood gurgling scream that I am sure the kids in school back in the caves could hear. Gerald was shaking with fear, and I smiled. Chuck continued brutalizing his enemy, slamming him in the ribs with some sort of axe, ripping chucks of flesh straight from his body. Boe jumped on him and ripped a good handful of flesh from the big man's lower kidney area. It was definitely a gory sight.

The other two were doing exactly the same; our enemies fell to their death at the hands of my mini platoon of men. This was too easy, and quite enjoyable if you ask me. I laughed hysterically as the two boys, Boe and Chuck, just demolished these men. They stood on top of their victory, giving themselves high fives and congratulatory praises on their accomplishment. Once the fight was over Chuck and his friends crawled their way up from the valley, hooting and hollering the whole way. I could tell this was their first real kill. Once we all sat around Jerold, I realized that he had passed out at some point during the fight. I had become so overwhelmed with the fight that I couldn't see that I had been squeezing tighter and tighter around Gerald's neck. We all had a good laugh and waited for him to wake up. For when he did...it could very well be the last moments he spends in this world, or any world at that matter.

CHAPTER SIXTEEN
"Who's running this show"

When Gerald woke up I slammed him with about a thousand questions, "Who are you working for, who knows we are coming, and did you possibly think you could drag us out here and we would just roll over and die?" "I swear guys, I didn't do anything. I just approved the route that was laid out; it looked the safest to me. I am with you guys, I swear it!" Gerald screamed trying to prove his innocence. His tears were convincing enough, but if I knew I was about to be gutted by five ruthless guys and a dog, I would be crying too.

"Number one... kid, who laid out this route?" Gerald's face got bright red as he continued screaming. "It came from higher. I haven't even left the caves before. How could I have drawn it? It was given to me! It's not my job to plan...just approve... I swear it! I don't know who planned it!" This kid sure does a lot of swearing. "Do you kiss your mother with that mouth you rat?" I asked as I pulled the rope I had been making for the past couple weeks out of my bag. I know a good way to get him to talk. He knows more than he is letting on, that's the least I can tell from his little charade. I tied a noose into my rope and slapped the loop around his neck, tightening it up all the way until his Adams apple was bulging on top of my roughly woven rope.

Gerald screamed for his life as I drug him to the edge of the cliff. Now, I am not good at judging distances, but I would say it's at least a good hundred foot drop to the bottom, and I know I had at least a good fifty feet of rope. With no quick snap on the end, the weight of his body against his neck is enough to cause a painful suffocating death. Gerald didn't even make it to the cliff's edge before he put two and two together and started spilling like a can of baked beans.

"Mr. Mason, Mr. Mason. It was Mason! He said I was to tell you this was my entire plan so you would trust me! So you could see that I was an asset to your team! I didn't plan anything, I was just told what to say. I promise you that I would never set you up, and I can prove it! All I did was take the crap maps I was provided, and draw a new one! I came with you why would I jeopardize my own life!" I dropped the rope immediately and removed it from his neck. Gerald continued to breathe heavily as tears fell from his eyes.

We all surrounded him, still unsure on whether or not he was trying to save his own skin, or if he was being truthful. From my experience in the field, I can tell whether or not someone is just telling me what I want to hear, or if he is really being truthful. And the fear in this kid's eyes didn't come from me, well partially me; I would like to think I can instill some sort of fear if I have to. But he was scared of something else, something bigger. Now I was curious and wanted to know more.

Why would Mason sabotage the freedom of his own people? This didn't make any sense. This is the same place that I was shot, which means I was on the lowers' territory still. There should not have been any hunting party here. Any way you slice it. This was a setup. "When did you realize that Mr. Mason wasn't rooting for the home team?" I asked him calmly. "I never did, he is the leader of our people Will, why would he do that? It doesn't make any sense. I figured at the most he was going to set you up on the way home to have you killed," Gerald was thinking out loud. Well, for once he got something right; it made no sense at all. Well, it made partial sense, I figured he would try and have me killed... but on the way home. Not on the first hit outside the gate. This made it seem like he didn't want the mission itself to succeed.

"Here are your choices Gerald. You can come with us, and finish the mission on our team this time, or... you can go home and tell the rest of the people what happened here, expose Mason to your people, and we will finish the mission...alone," I told him. I figured I could give him an out. If he went home, I knew he was in on it, and we shoot him. If I was dirty, I would leave. If he came with us, he was down for the cause, and could most likely be trusted.

But that still left the question as to how far the blame actually went. This could be bigger than just Mason. Did Cory know the truth? Is that why he didn't want me to go at the last second, because he knew we were going to be ambushed? There are too many questions and not near enough people to dangle over a cliff and answer them.

Jerold walked over to his pack and put it on his back, looking at the horizon that led towards the caves, and sighed. "I'm coming with you, Will, and I will prove to you I am not a traitor, whatever it takes. I have had a lot of questions about Mr. Mason and his actions. A lot of things don't add up. This might be my only shot at figuring out the real truth on why I have to live underground. The man has always been a little off and I have just been doing my job. I don't like this anymore than you do so let's go." He stepped off into the new direction and took the lead. Well, at least he will get shot first if we walk into anything else unexpected. The kid was right, he had a lot of proving to do and I will be watching him like a hawk.

Three hours into the walk we reached the outer limits of a city that was well marked on the map. The map said to outskirt this place, so I think we're going to stop for a few and take a breather. It seemed like a safe secluded area. Jerold begged to differ with my opinion and whined, "Uhm, this area is always raided by the rebels. I don't think that it is safe for us to be around. It is one thing to fight one Army. But if we get into it with two forces at once, I don't think our odds of survival will be very good at all." I have heard small talk about these rebel forces, and I for one would love to meet them. I am all for a rebel. Besides, Cory had mentioned that he was related to one of them.

Heavy wood line covered everything that the eye could see. A man could stay hidden in here for days. To the left of us, a good three hundred meters away, sat the town. There were no roaming guards floating around, no sentry's posted for a lookout, nothing. This town didn't even know we existed, and I wanted to keep it that way. "Does anyone need to stop and take a break?" I asked everyone, and everyone shook their head no. "Can we actually pick up the pace a bit, we're taking forever here," Chuck chimed in with his smartass tone that has become more prominent since the last battle.

"Well, yea we could but I didn't want to break you little girls off, so eat first. Two pieces of meat per man, and one canteen of water a piece as well. I want it done in ten minutes." I handed out the rations and watched them all pull their canteens out of their bags reluctantly. I felt like I had just told my kid he couldn't play anymore because we needed to go home. I didn't need any of them falling out from dehydration or hunger.

The next stop I will have them air out their feet, it is about that time. After everyone ate, we picked up and moved out into the new coming night. The suns were starting to set and I liked the night. We could move faster without being seen, make up for lost time at the bowling ball. We slowly made our way through the quiet town. There were only a few glowing lights in the windows of the buildings that lined the streets. These building looked like log cabins, some bigger than the others. I could tell this town had been assaulted a few times in the past. Door jams were splintered on abandoned homes and some of them were burnt and charred. No one had been here with negative intensions for a little while, so for right now it looks like no rebels.

It was late into the night when I felt the hair on the back of my neck stand up. That feeling you get when someone is watching you. I noticed that Boe had kept looking back as well. I halted the movement and took time out to listen. I heard nothing, but I am most definitely positive that we were being followed. I motioned for everyone to form a line and follow me into the heavier wood line. I was going to set up a three hundred and sixty degree perimeter about three hundred meters out, that way we can for sure see if we were being followed. If not, it would at least serve as a good resting point. We could all use a few hours of sleep. We had covered roughly twenty-five miles since the suns left us. The boys could definitely use some rest.

Once we were all formed up, I instructed them to get some sleep. Boe and I would take this watch; it wasn't like we hadn't done this before many times, just the two of us. The night was alive with crickets and coyotes. The sounds of nature were all around us, which is comforting in more ways than one. It meant that the surrounding wildlife had forgotten about us and started in their nightly rituals of singing songs to Mother Nature, and it meant that they would shut up if they heard anyone coming. That was one thing you could always count on out here. If you pay attention to your surroundings, you can find out when someone is coming long before you physically see them or hear them.

After three hours the suns had started to make their struggle back into the sky. I started to drift off to sleep with Boe leaned over my lap, when I heard it. The sound of silence was so loud that it made me wide awake in an instant. There wasn't a single sound in the woods anymore. Neither a cricket nor a bird chirp could be heard...complete silence. The silence that meant someone was following us. Twenty minutes later I saw three figures slowly and quietly making their way through the brush. There was one big man and two little men. Little men? Cave dwelling little men. There was definitely something going on, and I wanted to know what it was. They were clearly working together but why. Killing them was obviously a good option, and one that I favor personally. But this was too good of an opportunity to pass up. If I disable them, I can get information I want, and then kill them later. The big one was obviously for security purposes, so he isn't the one that needs to be breathing at the end of this. I have to figure out which of the two little men was in charge, or are they both important?

The three men were roughly one hundred and fifty meters away before I released my first poisoned arrow. The wind kicked in and sent my arrow into the big man's lower abdomen. This shot would kill him within ten minutes, so I had to act quickly. The second stun arrow flew straighter than the first, landing straight at the base of the spine of the man who turned to run, thus paralyzing him for further questioning. It's really a hindrance trying to hold a conversation with someone as they try to crawl away, this way is much more effective to have an attentive audience. The third arrow missed by half a foot and went straight through the neck of the last remaining man, sending him immediately to his death. Oh well, I have one little one and one big one. Surely between the two they are bound to be able to fill in some gaps. We can practice some team work and get some answers.

By the twang of my last arrow being released from my bow, the boys were up and running around trying to figure out what was going on. "Calm down fellows, we were being followed, which is why I holed us up here for the night. I wanted to double check and make sure we weren't alone, instead of guessing. I double checked and sure enough, we were followed and now they are in a very good position to give us some answers on who is playing ball on both sides of the fence. But we need to hurry because they won't last much longer. We have maybe five minutes left before they are gone; so let's go! Put on your angry faces, we have to mean business here; this may be our only chance at seeing who is behind all these shenanigans."

I gathered up my boys and we walked out to where my fallen enemy lay on the ground. "Hey, I know you know who I am, but I want to know who you are, and who sent you," I said calmly to the guy I had just shot in the stomach. He just stared at me cursing me up and down. This one had to weigh at least 300 pounds. "I ain't telling you anything, I guess you're just going to have to kill me," he told me in a defying sarcastic tone. I reached in and pulled out my knife. Fine, I'll kill him then. Before I could even step forward, Gerald jumped up and slammed his knife into the throat of the sarcastic beast of a man, and while twisting the handle, he pulled it out slowly and we watched as the life faded from his eyes.

"Wow, I can honestly say I did not see that one coming." I said as me and the other boys started laughing. Jerold was already pounding on the normal sized man's face, beating him to a pulp while yelling at him. "Who sent you here? Why would you do to this to your own people?" The little man just laughed at Jerold and refused to say a word, however I have to say he looked a little bit nervous from the throat cut we had all witnessed just seconds earlier. I can imagine though, all one hundred pounds of Gerald slamming you in the face wasn't enough to really convince you of anything. So I figured we would turn downright dirty. Why not, right?

I pulled my knife out and shoved it into his top arm...he screamed. So, apparently my test worked and he wasn't fully paralyzed. This works better in my favor anyways, now I can torture him into talking. I cut a slice out of the sweaty palm on his left hand...and he screamed. "We can do this the hard way, which I prefer... or the easy way until you start talking," I said. There was still no response from this guy. I'll give him this much, he is definitely a trooper. I gave Gerald the knife and let him go to town on this guy. Small, slow and deliberate stabs and cuts were administered to various parts of this man's body.

"Look, this will end when you tell me who sent you. I want to know what the heck is going on here, guy. You're already caught, your attempts to kill us are already foiled, so it's pointless to sit here and act like you're not going to tell us because...you will eventually tell us anyways. One way or another I am going to find out. And if I don't find out from you...I am going to kill you. Then, I am going to go back to the caves and kill everyone in your family. Moms, dads, brothers, sisters, cousins and I mean everybody. If you don't have any family, I'll burn down your house and kill your pets. If you don't have any pets I'll find you a gold fish, kill it and pin it to the wall to send a message. One way or another I will get "mine," rest assured," I told the dying man in front of me. "Did Q send you or Mason?" The man started laughing hysterically. "You still don't get it do you! You are a fool, all of you!" he said through his laughter and screams.

Gerald cut off his index finger, right hand. I was bent right over his face; just mere inches were between our eyes when I spoke to him. Gerald touched the blade to the little man's left index finger. This guy wasn't going to last much longer, so whatever I do I have to do it fast. "What don't I get...why don't you fill me in slick. Let me know what's going on and who sent you and I will patch you up and send you home alive." Still no answer from this guy just laughs and screams of pain. Gerald could tell I was beginning to become agitated, so he ripped that finger off which did the trick apparently, because between his squabbled cries, I could hear a 'Mr. Mason' in their somewhere, before he passed out.

"Ok, so I am pretty sure it is safe to say that Mason is behind all of this, which makes no sense whatsoever. So we're going to go home and ask him. I am going to take Boe and head up the road a mile or two, back towards the way we came, and see if there are any others." I walked off and motioned for Boe to come with me. The walk in the direction we had just passed was a quick one, only two sets of prints, no one else was following us. I can't figure out why Mason would go through these lengths to sabotage this mission. It was he, after all that came up with the ultimatum of helping them win their freedom or to die. If it was his idea why would he be against it all of a sudden? Why didn't he just tell me to not worry about it and send me home? Unless he was losing the vote of the people. They said they had become agitated with him due to his failures in attempts to free them or lack thereof. This means he would have to have an ultimatum for keeping them underground. But why would he have so much against me in the first place. This all seems a little much…a little too drastic. I turned to head back to the boys so we could leave.

Unless it was all Cory's idea, and he spread the word around camp telling everyone that I could free them. And once it was to that point Mason couldn't just dispose of me because then he would lose the town, because he killed their only shot at freedom. Come to think of it, I never saw Mason but twice, once when I got there and once when I left. He was built a little stockier than the rest of them, meaning he got out and around. He was tan, which meant he spent quite a bit of time in the sun. He couldn't be going out for diplomatic purposes if none of their people supposedly were even allowed outside of the caves. This would mean that Mason….is Q. He's running both sides. He keeps the smart ones underground hidden in fear, and the dumb ones up for some reason. I can't figure the politicking he has going on here, but if he is behind it, I am pretty sure he is actually playing the role of two people.

Cory had mentioned before that Mason was never really around, and was seldom seen when he was. So I am going to assume here that Mason sent me out to die. After a week or two when we don't show up, he would say we were killed and there was still no hope at a future. But that still kept the whole ordeal of the fuel and the ship in question, unless he was planning on using the ship for his own uses. I wish he would actually show up to America in a rickety old ship and get blown out of this world. That would be funny for sure. So the only thing I can think of is we need to go back and sneak in. We should grab up Cory first and find out what he knows, then sneak our way around and find Mason. Better yet, we will go back and hide out around the caves and wait for Mason to move out. He obviously comes and goes and not from the main entrance.

There are enough of us, we could spread out and just watch until we find out where he is coming from. The boys were already packed up, so we set out. All of these questions, and we still had no solid answers.

CHAPTER SEVENTEEN
"The long wait"

The path back to the bowling ball was much more difficult than earlier. I wasn't about to take a chance with our lives. We had to go back a different route to stay undetected. Once on the outskirts of the village, I noticed something a little different. There was a smell of smoke in the air...and stale blood. I raised my right hand up and formed a fist, motioning my boys to freeze in place. Slowly, I melted down to my knees and posted up behind a tree. I could barely see the village through the dense forest, but from what I could see, there had been trouble. I could see three bodies in the street stacked up together. I needed to get closer, because they look like big people. They look like upper people, and I didn't kill anyone in this town. Which means I am either being followed or this is mere coincidence. In my line of work, I don't believe in coincidence.

Creeping closer to get a better look, I spread my team out to be less noticeable. If we move in as one big gaggle, it's easier for someone to spot us. We needed to get closer and check out this situation. A few steps forward confirmed my guess. These were definitely three locals that had met their match. "Rebels," Gerald whispered to me from three tree's away. He pointed to a mark on the door that had been painted in blood. It appeared to be an A with a diagonal slash through it. I'm assuming this is the mark of the rebel forces Cory had spoke of earlier. As much as I really want to meet these guys, now is not the time or place. I can't afford to take the chance of making any more enemies here. Not now at least. I motioned for us to gather back up and head out.

Once outside of the village, Gerald spoke up, "I remember hearing something about a tree. I wasn't ever allowed into the meetings with his scouting parties. Well, any meetings to be quite honest with you. He said I wasn't quite there yet. But, I admit… I have eavesdropped from time to time. The word tree path has come up quite a few times." Chuck started whispering with his buddies. "Ok, what are you girls babbling about in your little circle of love?" I asked them.

Chuck spoke up for his group, "Well, we snuck out a few months ago to go check out the lake right. If you go up past the bluff and look towards our mountain, you can see a huge snarled dead tree that covers up an opening to the cave. We ain't ever been in there you see, but we have seen people come in and out of it. So, I would guess it is safe to say that is where Mason goes in and out unnoticed." Chuck has definitely proven himself to be an asset to the group.

"Well, looks like that is where we are going, good job boys!" I let Chuck and the boys take the lead, and me and Gerald took the rear, pulling security. With the Bowling Ball behind us, we were following Chuck's lead to the first snarled tree that he knew of. I figured it was better to take our time and stick together as one, seeing as we had no means of communication whatsoever. Chuck was leading us up to a high point bluff overlooking a side of the mountain that was hiding the caves, which housed those poor people inside. Those guys have never once thought they were being swindled by one of their own. Chuck pointed down the bluff to a well-worn path that led to a snarled tree right on the side of the mountain.

This guy sure wasn't worried about hiding his tracks. He was pretty arrogant if you ask me. I can't wait to smoke this dude. These people had to be pretty ignorant to let one man run everything on this planet. I couldn't help but hope that there is another continent somewhere here, and they go all explorer-mode and take over this land. That would be priceless.

" Gerald, I want you to go back in and tell everyone that you were the only one that made it, we were cut down a long way away from here. Talk to Cory, but remember *no one* can be trusted, find out if he is with us, or against us. I want you to gather as much information as you can. See if you can touch base with Mason. I am sure he is dying to know that we finally failed. However, I doubt he is expecting your survival. Make it look good and act like you knew he was dirty the whole time and your fine with it. Like I said, no one can be trusted here. We don't know who all is involved, but we need to find out. See if you can figure out when Mason is leaving again, but be sneaky about this. I am sure they will kill you if they find out what you know. Speaking of which, we can't have you walking in there just dirty with a little blood on your hands, you're going to need to go in there in pretty bad shape, after all...you're the lone survivor right? So, I am sorry for this." I stopped mid-sentence and punched Gerald straight in the face, dropping him onto his rear. The rest of the boys caught on quick and we all took turns beating Gerald with every ounce of strength we had left. Boe even got a few snips in. I won't lie, I kind of feel sorry for him, but this way it would be more believable. We need it to be believable. Gerald's life depended on it.

Gerald swelled up like a balloon almost instantly and we all laughed, including Gerald, when we were done. I think I accidentally knocked out one of his teeth. "All for a good cause man; go in there and make me proud. Make them believe it. Don't take forever either, I want you back out here in two days tops, ok?" I gave Gerald a hug and sent him on his way. What can I say, I am still a hugger. We watched as Gerald disappeared into the scenery that led towards the main entrance of the cave, it was maybe only a mile or so. I couldn't help but hope that he makes it in and out safely.

"Well boys, here comes the boring part. We sit here and wait. We will take turns on shifts at this point, we're looking for anyone coming out of that pass right there. I am pretty positive that this will be the entry and exit point for Mason and his guys. He is too arrogant to come up with different routes. I am sure he isn't expecting anyone to question him, but his time will come. In the meantime, while one of you are watching, I'm going to teach the other three how to fish. I have yet to see anyone out here eat fish, and fish is good if fried up right." Everyone was excited and slightly relieved to the outcome of the events this past week.

This was easier on us; it was just the simple matter of proving it to the people. We would have to put him on display and hope he doesn't have a secret army of people inside of the caves that would kill us when we walked in with him tied up and beaten. That was going to be our only option, prove to the people that he is the real reason they aren't allowed outside. Once they realize that they have been swindled, I would have to turn the community over to someone, and hope that they do the right thing.

One of Chuck's friends, who don't ever talk much, so I couldn't even tell you his name, took the first watch. I led Chuck and his two buddies down to the lake which was half a mile behind us, away from the caves. We were going to be a few days out here at least, so I had some time to try and enjoy myself before my trip home. Plus, it wouldn't hurt to get to know the rest of the crew. "What are your names?" I felt really bad not knowing any of their names. "I am John Boy, I was wondering when you were going to ask me that." We all started laughing as I started to gather up long strips of weeds and shredding them down to thin strings. "And I am Hank, man." The second boy chimed in. "I like Hank. Back in my world, the best singer in the world is named Hank. That's a good name," I replied.

I watched as the three boys did everything I did, making their own lines. I didn't even know if we were going to catch anything, but it's always worth a try. There was really no reason for us all to stay up there on watch. I took some bone fragments from my pocket and started handing them out, just little slivers of deer bone that I had planned on carving at one point or another. They should make a fine hook for our cane poles. It took about 10 pieces of bone and five hours, but we finally all had made our perfect hook. I explained the theory behind catching a fish. Come to find out, none of them had ever even tried this before. They didn't even know that fish were edible. Kind of made me laugh since Native Americans back home, before modern civilization would eat or smoke just about anything. These people had not even tried fish. Hell, one of the first food items on the menu were fish and corn. This place still never ceases to amaze me.

Once we tied off our homemade lines and hooks to the end of the sticks we had found, we set off hunting for bait. "Worms usually make good bait if you don't have anything else. I don't really see anything hitting the top of the water, so I am going to assume that there is a bunch of catfish down there eating off the bottom. You can use any type of insect really. But the best bait for fishing like this will be something you can throw on the bottom of the water and wait for something to pick it up... like this," I explained. I was digging a hole near the water's edge under a shade tree. It was really a prime time spot because I held up a huge ungodly night crawler for all to see.

I showed them how to bait a hook, and they did. We all spread out and dropped our lines in the water and waited...and then waited some more. We weren't getting as much as a single bite and I was becoming quite irritated because I wanted to fry up some fish somehow. I have been craving a good catfish fry for a while now. We waited for what seemed like hours, when Chuck's pole nearly jerked out of his hands. Chuck had no idea what to do. He actually looked scared for once. "Will, what's going on? Is this supposed to happen?" He screamed at me. I yanked the pole out of his hands and landed a good size fish that looked very similar to a catfish. I felt like I was taking my kids out fishing for the first time. Bright smiling faces when they finally caught something and then boredom when they weren't biting.

CHAPTER EIGHTEEN

"Fish in the fry"

We had caught about five good size catfish when I decided to call it quits and figure out exactly how I was going to cook the fish without having a pan. "I can grind out a rock and make it look like a pan, and I bet I can do it in under an hour!" Hank declared as he ran out of sight to go find a good candidate for a pan. I dug through my pack and found a bag of the flour like substance that Cory rarely uses to cook with, and pulled out a few chunks of the fat I trimmed off the hog that the boys had caught. You know it still amazes me that they have this stuff which is basically flour, just not all purified like back home, but it works the same. Yet they don't have any sugar or sweetener of any kind, which would be all the makings I would need to conjure up some good cookies. Oh well, maybe someday. I didn't see any sugar cane floating around, so I would be of no help anyways trying to explain to them this simple process of cookie making.

Sure enough, maybe half an hour had gone by and Hank came running up with a perfectly sized make shift pan. Apparently he had grinded out the middle of the rock with something, but he wasn't saying what. Don't ask don't tell, right? I started a little fire near the edge of the water and behind a tree, as to hide most of the smoke. I shaved off some good fat shavings and started throwing them in the pan, letting them melt down to make grease. It wasn't really working out like I had envisioned, but oh well; it will work all the same.

John Boy and Chuck chimed in bantering back and forth with Hank, making fun of him for his homemaking skills. "Maybe we should trade you for my neighbor's sister, she can make pans out of nothing too, you know. But she has a better right hook than you. So, while you are at home cooking for her mom and cleaning, maybe little sis could be out here pulling her own weight," John Boy spit out between laughs. Hank punched him in his arm and John Boy and Chuck held Hank down wrestling with him. It had been a long time since I had seen guys making fun of each other and horse playing. I have to admit I missed it.

I wonder if there are any grasses or spices that taste good floating around here. "Hey boys, I'll be back shortly. Tend to the fire and watch out for your guy up there on the hill. Start cutting this fish up and peel the skin off, watch out because those fins will cut your finger off if you're not careful. Cut here at the belly to clean out the inside, and you should have the meat left after that. Remember, you can pull the skin off of this fish like you do on an animal. It's not scaly. I will be back in like ten minutes or so," I instructed, as I took off down the trail tasting everything I could touch. I started to make my way back to the top of the ridge to check on our sentry and make sure he was doing ok. It had been about four hours, so I figured I would relieve him for a bit, seeing as he has been sitting in a nice patch of different style grasses that I could try out.

"Hey bud, I never caught your name." The kid looked up at me and studied my face for a second. I couldn't tell if I had offended him by not speaking to him this whole trip. "The name is Jeremy. We have had a lot going on, no time really for introductions. Aint shit going on up here." He said as he stood up and stretched out his back and arms. "Alright Jeremy, go ahead and head down there. Get ready for some chow, send chuck up here to take your place." Just like that he was gone. I looked out over the clearing and could perfectly see the tree entrance. It really was a beautiful scene. I stood on top of a valley filled with wildlife and flowers. Sporadic rocks stood up against the horizon the closer it got the caves. The mountain was about three quarters of a mile out. We should have plenty of time to react when we see someone coming out. I sniffed out a few more good leaves and plants that had a good hint of spice to them. These will do perfectly. I'm not making a gourmet meal by any means but flavor is a must with me.

By the time that Chuck had made it up to me on the ridge, I had already acquired all of the spices that I wanted to use for the fish fry and I was sure that the grease was good and hot. "Alright Chuck, it's your watch now. I'll bring you some food when it is done. Four hour shifts, so I'll send someone else up to replace you in a few," I instructed Chuck, who solemnly nodded and sat down at the edge of the bluff, taking up his post. I headed down the hill and saw the other three boys fighting in the lake, Boe nipping at their heels half submerged in the water. It was good to see people acting like people for once. I closed my eyes and listened to the sounds of laughter and water lapping against the rocky shore. I could almost hear the sound of my wife laughing at a joke her brother was bound to tell at one point or another. The smell from my camp fire smelled vaguely of the burning oak that I am for sure is burning at a campfire right now in Kansas somewhere, no doubt. It was so peaceful and so serene; it almost brought a tear to my eye.

"Will, I just saw Mason go into the caves. He came from the direction we had come from. I say we sit down and wait on Jerold to figure out what's going on inside. Then we go in there and kill that sorry excuse of a man, free the people, and then you flee the coop." Chuck's voice had slammed into my mind, interrupting my memories. I nodded in agreement to Chuck, whom was apparently doing his job better than I was. Apparently I was lost in memory lane and didn't see anything or anybody. Chuck definitely had the same thought process as I did, and I enjoyed that about the kid. Ever since he pretty much stalked me to death, I had always felt some type of connection with him. It was almost like that little brother type of bond. A hate-love relationship if you will. He was smart though, and I will give him that. He always seemed to have the right things going through his mind at the right time and place.

Sitting by the fire, the wind blew slightly down from the top of the hill. As I slipped the pieces of fish filet into the popping grease, the smell of the savory meat felt as if my taste buds were getting drop kicked in the knees by a kangaroo. We hadn't eaten a real hot meal in a few days and it was definitely time for one now. Gerald should be back by tomorrow and soon we would be on the move, our last move hopefully. I won't lie; I don't have all the faith in the world in Gerald. He may be a solid kid, but he doesn't seem to be the strong willed tough guy type...clearly. The other three guys had that rebellious attitude that I love to see in people.

Society everywhere has adopted what they call "normality's amongst the community." What a certain group of people say is the right way to live and the right way to think, and then they enforce it with huge penalties. Then, there is the small group of people that stand up and just say no. They fight back against the conformist, and that keeps me employed... and happy. I must admit that I am somewhat of a rebel myself, and this is what linked us all together. It just amazes me that even though we could be from two different worlds, quite literally might I add... we can share so many similarities.

The food we had eaten had somehow casted a deep sleep amongst us all, including Boe. I could hear his heavy deep breaths in the darkness. It could be due to the fact that no one had really eaten in a while, so we all over indulged ourselves and became victim of the notorious head nod. John Boy seemed to be the only one that was still wide awake. "John Boy, go replace Chuck up on the lookout and I will come get you at first light," I hollered over the fire. He was busy throwing rocks at his sleeping buddy. He agreed and ran off into the night. I could no longer fight the urge to fall into a deep coma for a few hours. Resistance was pointless. The light crackling and popping of the fire lulled me into a deep, memory filled slumber...until I was awakened by the quiet.

CHAPTER NINETEEN
"Betrayal"

There are two different types of quiet in this world, the good kind and the bad kind. This was definitely not the good kind. There were no bugs rustling, the fire was no longer crackling and my ears where ringing with a vengeance trying to strain and hear anything. I strained my eyes against the dark moonless night and could see Boe standing rigid against the horizon, gleaming up to where John Boy is pulling guard duty. The other kid wasn't anywhere around. It took everything I had to pull myself out of my comfortable position I had somehow found in the middle of the night and started making my way up the hill. Everyone was gone. I looked over where we had stored all of our packs. Nothing. Panic hit me. I could see all the way around our hole, even down to the cave entrance. No one. They had all seemed to disappear without any trace of a struggle. Their packs were gone, and I was the only one who was left. Could I have been so foolish that I let these boys bamboozle me into a trap? I didn't know any of them aside from Chuck from a hole in the ground. No sign of a struggle, Boe didn't freak out, so they straight up left.

One thing was for sure, I couldn't stay here. Boe seemed to be sniffing the ground and pausing every few feet looking as puzzled as I was. I am sure he felt the same way that I did. Betrayed. "Don't worry about it son, they ain't here, and in two minutes neither will we," I told Boe as I headed back down to grab my pack and disappear. Whatever was going on, I will not be caught with my pants down. I'm moving locations. "Find them," I whispered to Boe after I had got everything I needed. I followed him as he stuck his nose to the ground and struck up a trail. It didn't take long to realize we were going straight into the cave we had been watching.

Once at the entrance, Boe hesitated for a second. I loaded a poison arrow into my cross bow and gave him the nod to go ahead. The cave was dark and drafty, just wide enough for two people to stand side by side. The ceiling was not more than three feet above my head. I couldn't help but feel slightly claustrophobic. The passage opened up around a corner into a large room that was dimly lit with torches. The lighting here was horrible. Good for me, but not very good for someone trying to see what was going on and where. My heart skipped a beat as I saw the dim outline of a huge black shadow in the center of the cave. Could this really be what I think it is? I crept a little bit closer, stepping away from the wall and into the center of the cavern. If I was to guess I would say that the main cavern was roughly one hundred and fifty meters wide and two hundred meters long. The top was black, so I couldn't even tell how high up it was. What seemed like a thousand feet up I could see a dim silhouette of an opening. Like a volcano.

The sunlight started to seep in from the opening, still not providing me much illumination. This place reminded me of a volcano. Even with the morning light seeping in from well over five hundred feet in the air, I could still barely make out the room. Creeping closer to the center of the cavern, my heart officially dropped. There she was in all her glory.... Dixie. My ship. She was definitely a sight for sore eyes. I couldn't help the feeling of wanting to run in, press go, and hope for the best. There were too many odds at stake. There could be no fuel, which would just prove embarrassing and fatal to me. I don't like either of those repercussions, and there is still the matter at hand on what happened to Chuck and the boys. Did they betray me, or were they taken captive? I couldn't with a good conscience just up and leave, not knowing the truth. What if they were taken and I was their only hope for survival, those poor boys...I already lost one team on this planet, I don't really feel like losing another.

Ok, mission at hand here is going home. Not the safety of these people, nor Chuck. Home. Wife and kids. Home...my own thoughts were drowned out by the vague recollection of the night before when the boys were splashing in the water. The people here needed help, and God put me here for a reason. For once I can make a positive difference in someone's life. I apparently am growing soft in my old age. There is no way they betrayed me. They had to of been taken captive and led them away from where I was sleeping. How could I not have heard them?

I waited about five minutes before pressing on, giving my eyes time to adjust to the new atmosphere of the room. There appeared to be cells on the far chamber of the room. I couldn't see inside of them, but that's where I was headed. If they are empty I am out of here. Scaling the walls and staying in the dim outskirts of the cavern walls, Boe and I made our way to the first cell...empty. Three cells down there was a huddled figure in the far corner. I couldn't make out the face, but I knew immediately that it was Chuck. What a relief, my boy was captured. Well, relief that he didn't betray me, but sucks for him at the same time.

"Psstt. What ya in for, killer?" I whispered through the dark. I have done my fair share of time myself, so I know how it feels to be locked up. That lonesome feeling of hopelessness that you get when you are behind bars never disappears until you are safe and free. I haven't been to jail in years and had no intentions on going back any time soon. Chuck's head shot up and he ran to the front of the cell. I could see tears in his eyes... his freshly blackened eyes. Whoever grabbed him definitely didn't take him easy. Dried blood still clotted up along the ridges of his massive knuckles. At least he put up a fight. I could tell he was still on my side and that lifted a heavy weight off my shoulders. The cell was roughly ten feet deep and maybe 4 foot wide max. No more than five feet separated the roof from the floor. Chuck had to be bent at the waist to walk around without hitting his head. It had appeared that a group of inmates that had escaped from Alcatraz had taken all their spoons and cut these cells out of the walls of these caves. This definitely was no professional job. Somehow the doors itself, bars and all, seemed to be carved of stone with a small opening for viewing and eating. Not large enough to fit a head or shoulders through though. A lock secured the door that swung heavy on its hinges. A lock that looked pretty easy to pick, given you had a paper clip or two, which I just so happen to have, as I try never to leave home without it.

Chuck was breaking through my concentration with an eager hushed yet rushed ecstatic voice, "Will, you have to go man. Get out of here! We were set up, both of us. Those bastards jumped me while I was sleeping and took me here. All three of them, I have known them for years man! I can only assume that Gerald is involved in this as well. They said they are going to kill me for treason and helping the enemy, and no one will be the wiser since I no longer have any family left alive. I don't know what to do man...but they also said they were going out to kill you at first light and tell everyone you were in bed with the bad guys and were playing us all along...they will be back here soon, so you need to go and get out of here. Your ship is right there man, they fueled it already. Get in it and go." I could barely hear everything that Chuck was telling me in a hoarse whisper, but I got the gist of it. I was a free man if I jump in the driver's seat and hit go. Sounds like a great plan but I am not going anywhere without Chuck.

CHAPTER TWENTY
"Who are you really"

I looked up the cavern walls and try to figure if the ship will fit out of the hole at the top. I would assume so, they wouldn't put it right here for no reason. I would have to take the chance. I could do this right now. I could be out of here! Stephanie, the kids and everyone else I loved was within arm's reach. They don't have anything strong enough to penetrate the hull of this ship once I was in. The hairs on the back of my neck stood up immediately and Boe began to snarl. I spun around stopping a giant club from connecting to the back of my skull. "Not today! AGHHHH!" I let out a rebel yell that echoed throughout the caverns. I grabbed this man's throat and sank my small fingers behind his oversized Adams apple. Every passion that I have ever felt in my life seemed to pour out of every pour of my body. It felt as if my toes were even screaming in anger. My wife's face slammed in the front of my mind...her tears. The pain of me not being there for her. I twisted my hand ripping his throat right out of his neck; blood splattered the walls in a sickening *schplat*.

My adrenalin began to rush as if three million bats had been flushed out of there dark hide out. From my toes to the top of my skull, I had reached the breaking point that I have always avoided. I was officially out of control. I grabbed the dead man's face and began to slam it with a rock until his left eye was lying near my feet, still attached to his skull. Three more men ran out into the main cavern at me from the right corridor and I could hear more piling in from all around me. I knew this was the end, there clearly is no way out but I wasn't giving up. I am this close to a fueled ship home. A green button push and I am the hell out of here. Dead or alive I am going home, with or without my dignity intact. I rushed through all of the guys pockets and found what I was assuming to be the key to Chuck's cell. I could barely keep my hands steady from all of the adrenalin.

I sprinted the five feet across to Chuck's cell and threw the key in. *TWICK.* The lock sprang open with Chuck's forceful kick, knocking me on my rear. The screams were everywhere, there had to be over two dozen people in this cave coming for us. "Get Boe and get to the ship, or just get the hell outta here boy!" I screamed over all the anger and confusion. "No, Will. Let's go together! Follow me!" Chuck scrambled into the darkness with Boe right on his heels. I felt the rush of clubs and sticks being swung at my face. I grabbed my knife off the belt of my pants and just started slashing. It was still so dark in this room I can't even see three feet in front of my own face. Every swing felt like your first kiss. The rush of new emotions, excitement and revenge all in one. The connect was as rewarding as losing your virginity, immediately producing a satisfying cocky smile across the lips of some hormone raged teen boy. This was the night this charade ended. Dead or alive I am done tonight. I could hear Chuck fighting his way out of the corridor, it sounded like he made it out of the main cavern. I was so scared for him, he didn't deserve to die. He was just a kid.

I felt the sharp sting of something melting through my flesh like that of a knife cutting through a warm stick of butter. I didn't care, all I can feel is pressure. I have been forced into doing a lot of things before in my lifetime, but dying is not one of them. A quick toss of the knife landed halfway through a man's rib cage. I jumped over one's back to retrieve my knife from its temporary home, twisting while removing would indeed prove a kill. And that's all I want to do...kill. A twist on a neck proved that these people had weak bones. Their weakness was my strength. It fueled me. I fought for what seemed like hours. Grabbing, pulling, biting, tearing and screaming. I lost count of how many times I had a good hit delivered by a fist or a club to my face. The room got darker with every flash of light that followed an immediate blow to my face. It was like a horrible lightning storm with no end. A good thump hit the back of my head, while a quick bright flash of light pounded the backs of my eyes. Bodies lay scattered across the floor, I didn't know how much longer I was able to last.

I took the fight to the ground. It didn't matter how many people were on me. It doesn't make a difference. I would prefer to fight in three to one odds anyhow. You can only do so much, and I was trained. They were not. I easily snagged ankles, snapping them like a brittle pretzel underneath the fingers of an unforgiving three year old. I must have gone through a dozen ankles when the last flash of lighting paralyzed my entire body and I stopped. I couldn't even say anything, I could just breathe…barely… and look through the bodies of the men and see my ship, Dixie. She stood there gleaming in the morning light that had made its way into the top of the cavern that I could see clearly now was cut out like a volcano. The opening was big enough for Dixie to slip through and take me home.

I felt the emotion flood through me again, starting at the calves and slowly rising into the bottom pit of my stomach. Two of them were lying on my back keeping my chest pinned to the floor, while three others firmly held my feet. I could feel nothing but defeat. And this was worse than any pain I had known before. As the room lit up with more light from the suns I could see at least thirty men laying either dead or crawling on their hands and knees. I had done damage, but not well enough. I could not see Chuck or Boe anywhere. I know I had told them to leave me and get out, but I still felt abandoned. I hope that boy makes it out and frees his people. I also hope they are at least going to kill me and not throw me in a cell. I couldn't handle being put into a cell, I would rather face death.

I could feel my foot twitch, the life was slowly starting to creep back into my limbs. The adrenalin was rising again. I started to laugh. And then I felt nothing. No pressure, no one on my back at all. I rolled over to my back and looked up and saw Mason walk in the room ordering them all away from me. Mason looked around the room with a slightly astonished and sarcastic smile on his face. He started clapping his hands in a sarcastic matter as if to applaud my show. He didn't carry himself the same any more. He had arrogance about him, which is something I wanted to remove from him immediately. "Lock him up; let him suffer through his pains for the day. No food or water. Kill him in the morning…put him in the cell facing his ship. Make sure he looks at it. I want him to feel the pain he has caused me. That will teach him to die when I want him to," Mason barked out to his little group of henchmen. What little group of henchmen he had left.

My heart sank immediately. "By the way, Will. She is fueled and ready to go as promised. I am a man of my word." He laughed hysterically. "Who in the hell do you think you are you foolish boy. Do you have any idea who in the hell I am? This is my world! I created it this way and I can do with it what I see fit. You thought you could run in here and be all patriotic and just change things? I am what you call a leader...Untouchable...I ran one of the largest corporations on earth single handedly..." "Belver?" I hoarsely whispered up to him. "But your dead." Silence filled the air and a small group near me started laughing. "Dead is an earth thing my friend...clearly I'm alive and doing quite well for myself might I add." Belver's laughter was so maniacal it made me sick. He was so proud of himself. "How did you beat the cancer?" I asked him clearly he wanted to tell the story before he offed me...so I might as well die with closure. "Ah yes, you see. It was quite brilliant. We showed up here looking for diamonds and instead found...you know what Will. Don't concern yourself with any more of my affairs. I would be more concerned as to what awaits you when I get back from my meeting in a few hours." Belver's laughter struck up again as he exited the caves.

I was so tired I couldn't even muster out a smart ass reply. I couldn't even open my mouth. The taste of blood...a mixture of a battery and salty syrup ran down my throat if I even tried to grunt. Three of the men started walking over to me laughing. If they think they are locking me behind a closed door they are sadly mistaken. The anger swelled up inside of me and gave me that last oomph I needed to move. I grabbed the stick that was lying to the guy on my right and swung at an ankle, only to have a forty pound rock slammed on my left knee, crushing it instantly. The tears welled up and blinded my vision. I felt that one. I felt as if a semi-truck had slowly parked on my knee, bending it into an unnatural position. The pressure on my knee was immense and unbearable.

I was blacking out and coming to at the same time. The pain I was feeling in my entire body immediately set in. It was excruciating to say the least. The throbbing and aching never stopped. The light would flash in and out as I could feel myself being drug into the same cell that Chuck was in.

The closer I got to the cell, the more fear rose inside of me. I can't do it. This was the worse feeling ever. The door slammed behind me and there I was, back at seventeen, lonely, cold and betrayed. Well, the knee cap being shattered was pretty bad and pulled a pretty close second I must say. I am pretty sure if I had a cookie right now...yeah...no, it wouldn't help at all. I will never make it home. My ship lay glistening in the sunshine like a sexy supermodel no more than fifty feet in front of my cage. She seemed to be mocking me. All of this way and I give up. So close yet so far away. The hours seemed to fly by as I watched the suns disappear on the other side of the opening.

People took turns coming by my cell and either laughing at me or spitting on me. I no longer cared. It was just a countdown to the end of my life anyways. Not that I had a watch on or anything. All of the things I have taken for granted seemed ridiculous at this point. All of the unnecessary fights, the nights of getting stupid drunk and ending up in jail. Pointless moments that I had wasted away, pissed into the wind if you will. I fell asleep after four hours of staring at the ship.

TWICK.

The sound immediately has awoken me from my painful slumber. Finally my hour had come, all of this for nothing. I couldn't see anything in the night, my eyes were swollen shut. I could no longer move my limbs; it was as if every arm weighed three hundred pounds. I heard footsteps all around me and my heart began to race out of control. I couldn't believe that this was what it was like to die alone. My biggest fear was finally becoming a reality. The hurt and pain wouldn't stop. At least this was the end. No more wondering if I was going home or not, this is definitely the "not" part. I will not go out embarrassing myself or my country. I gathered all the energy left in my body and muttered through swollen shut lips... "You gotta hit a man when he aint lookin' huh. Do your worst."

I could still feel the blood rushing out of my mouth and nose and slowly draining into the back of my throat. Just to try and spit it on the ground hurt so bad. "What are you in for ol' timer?" a soft voice broke through the painful silence. I could feel the tears welling up behind my eyes. I felt Boe's wet nose touch my cheek and could feel the broad shoulders of Cory as he lifted me onto his back. Gerald was in the back ground whispering for them to hurry. "We got you, Will; everything is going to be ok." I could hear Chuck whisper into my ear as we made our way down a passageway going deeper into the mountain. The air grew colder and I could tell Cory was leading the way. We weren't going out, we were going in deeper.